SUPER

Ernie Lindsey

Publisher's Note: This is a work of fiction. Names, characters, places, and incidents are a product of the author's imagination. Locales and public names are sometimes used for atmospheric purposes. Any resemblance to actual people, living or dead, or to businesses, companies, events, institutions, or locales is completely coincidental.

ISBN-13: 978-1500230760
ISBN-10: 1500230766

Super / Ernie Lindsey. -- 1st ed.

For Sarah and Jack.

More than super.

ONE

Present Day

The woman from South Korea looks fetching in a white pantsuit. Her hair is the color of a raven, flecked with rainy day gray, and she wears it cropped close and level like a '50s flattop.

Out of everyone in this godforsaken support group, I trust her the least. In fact, I couldn't trust her *less* if I tried; yet, I'm starting to think that she's not the reason I'm here.

Still, she's got some nerve.

John Conklin carries doughnuts around the circle, and when he asks in a hushed voice if I want glazed or Boston Crème, I politely decline. I know where his hands have been. "Suit yourself," he says. "They're from that gluten-free place up near Powell's."

"Patsy's?"

His eyes light up. "Yeah, that one!"

I reassure him that, indeed, I do not want a doughnut, though on most days, I'd give my right arm for their blessed pastries. Bottom line, I don't want John Conklin anywhere near my food.

Dallas works that Cheshire grin on her face, lying to everyone in the room, claiming that she's responsible for Patriotman's death off the coast of the Maldives.

We're supposed to be here for that cotton-candy bullshit: love, support, understanding, and a shoulder to cry on. We're not here to beat our chests about past conquests.

I should clarify: *they're* here for that reason. I'm here for my own.

While the world mourns the death of the man in red, white and blue tights, from New York, to Shanghai, to Cairo, with newspapers screaming their headlines of despair, I sit here smoldering inside because I know the truth.

Plus, a woman named Kimmie Strand has been all over the news, talking to whomever she can, claiming to be the only witness.

Whatever. I repeat. I know the truth.

Dallas is lying, but that doesn't mean she's my culprit.

She sips her steaming mug of green tea and says, "You know I can't tell you where the body is, Charlene. That would defeat the entire purpose. Imagine the hysteria."

Charlene—she's the attractive redhead—

congratulates my South Korean counterpart and hugs her handbag closer to her chest. Her paranoia issues far outweigh my own manufactured problems, and the rest of us had begun to speculate that we'd never see her again. The fact that she's here, that she made it again, says more about her character than I care to admit because she's still a suspect. I like Charlene, no doubt, but if it comes down to a cup of coffee or handcuffs—not the furry kind—I'm choosing duty over desire.

Dallas goes on and on about her methods and tactics. She's such a braggart that I'm beginning to wonder why she's even here in the first place. She doesn't belong. Neither do I, but I don't care that she suffers from compulsive lying. I don't like her.

"He was right there, guys. I'm telling you, just ripe for the plucking, and I was in and out before he took a second breath. Not that he would've had a chance to, mind you."

Lie.

"Of course I was sure he was dead before I left. Don't you all double check?"

Lie. Lie.

"I got the liquid brozantium wholesale. I'll see if my supplier wants me to pass his card around."

Damned lie.

The only thing she's gotten right is the fact that they don't know where the body is.

I do.

How do I know she's not telling the truth about the rest of it?

Because that gig was *my* handiwork. A week ago, the world learned that Patriotman was eliminated with a simple medicine dropper full of liquidized brozantium, delivered to the ear canal. Every major news outlet on the planet received word that he'd died on the aptly named yacht, *Misery's Fortune*.

The only known witness was a woman— apparently a (*ahem*) friend of Patriotman's—who saw it from a hiding spot in the main cabin.

I wonder if she's been enjoying her time in the spotlight. I may need to pay her a visit.

The story goes that some top secret, ultra clandestine government organization paid an assassin (*yours truly*) to get rid of the dear Commander, and *voila*, one dead superhero, as ordered. Everybody knows that he was vulnerable to brozantium, but a single, concentrated dose that close to the brain? Dude never had a chance.

The thing is, see, people had been trying to send the man of chiseled chest-diamonds to his grave for decades, but they were going about it all wrong; the trick was to get in there where he was vulnerable.

Hell, I can't think of any good examples right now—okay, say it's like Luke Skywalker and the Death Star. Patriotman's ear canal could be that opening that Skywalker flies into and then fires his *pew-pew* proton torpedoes or whatever. Anyway, we all know how *that* ended.

Am I proud of it? Damn straight.

I mean, I guess I am. Patriotman had done a lot of good for the world, and it was a shame, but *come on*! On the surface, as the world sees it and will never, ever know, I accomplished something that *no other person in history* has been able to do. More people have walked on the moon.

There's a part of me that wants to say, "Good riddance," because it's the end of an era. New book, new story, new chapter. A world that will learn to be self-reliant on the other side of Patriotman's death.

Dallas says, "Tara, there's simply no way—I'm sorry, *Mara*—there's no way I'm going to offer you any legitimate proof and reveal my sources. We all know how this works."

Mara crosses her legs and her arms. She pouts until Charlie Delta tries to put a hand on her shoulder. She squirms away with an upturned lip.

Dallas says, "Well, he certainly didn't die with his boots on—*wink, wink*."

I understand what she means, but, gag me with a spoon if she's insinuating what I think she's insinuating.

Here's the problem: I have no way to refute this woman. She can sit there and lay claim to Patriotman or any of my other conquests like Gray Ghoul, Scarlet Gargoyle, Captain Kane, Deathmarch, Quickstrike, Sam Diamond, the entire Power Hour Team, and even the *Crimson* Gargoyle, and nobody would know the difference.

I'm bound by contractual obligation to keep my damn mouth shut—the US government doesn't look kindly on its subcontractors sharing state secrets—and she gets all the glory, at least among our counterparts.

In fact, if she signed the same agreements I did, then she's in clear violation of subparagraph three, section four point two. Forget what it says, but if I had a mind to tattle, she'd be up a certain creek without a certain boat propulsion device.

Should I care? No. Do I? Bah, whatever.

It's *ridiculous*, and I'm tempted to call her out in front of this entire gaggle of heathens, but who will believe me? Dallas has clout among this den of miscreants and, supposedly, I'm just here for the anxiety issues.

What I'm doing with this gathering of mentally imbalanced, professional assassins is another story that I'll get to in a minute, but first, let me offer a little background.

We meet every Tuesday and Thursday in the back of a bowling alley that smells like stale beer and floor cleaner. I'm always worried about being congregated here with nearly everyone of my ilk.

If Billie Bombshell happened to learn about this highly clandestine meeting, she could swoop in, drop one of her explosive devices on the roof, and ninety percent of the world's elite superhero assassins would vanish.

She swore her vengeance after I eliminated her brother, Billy Barbell, but if I took the time to worry about everyone who wants retribution at my expense, I'd be a quivering mess like Charlene.

Remember how in *Forrest Gump* all the shrimping boats were destroyed, and that left the spoils to Forrest? If somebody blew up this building right now, our few remaining colleagues left out there would have more work than they could handle.

The owner, this wrinkled raisin of a guy named Jeff, is a retired NSA agent himself, so he doesn't mind

if the twelve of us gather and whine about how hard
our lives are, travelling all over the world to beautiful,
exotic locations so we can purge superheroes as
various governments deem fit. They have their reasons.
I ask, they tell me, and more often than not, I'm happy
to comply. The bastards deserve it.

'If the price is right, no job is too small or too light.'

That's my motto. Sure, the rhyming is hokey, but it
makes it simple to remember me, and I'm partly
convinced that's why I get more jobs than some of
these other jokers. I thought about getting it embossed
on a stack of business cards and changed my mind.
You don't want a paper trail in this line of work.
Literally and figuratively.

Anyway, back to the support group and this ratty
bowling alley. I'd prefer a bagel shop, but a certain
amount of discretion is required when you do what we
do for a living.

On the plus side, Jeff also allows us to roll a few
free games, and I have to admit, my skills have gotten
better over the past month. I broke a hundred last
week for the first time ever. John Conklin—he of the
doughnuts, who is also the demented bastard with a
necrophilia addiction—nearly rolled a perfect game a
couple of weeks ago. I'll never forget the look on his
face when that final 10-pin didn't fall, and if the guy

humped something other than dead superheroes, I might be able to find a dash of sympathy for him.

I mean, damn, one pin away from a perfect game. Can you imagine?

Sorry, was that too callous? I've been at this a while, and I've seen shit that would make Stephen King cringe, so you'll have to excuse my forays into *not-giving-a-crap* insensitivity. It's natural to me at this point. You have to adopt a thick shell of armor or you'll never get through the day.

Okay, so I mentioned there are twelve of us: Dallas, Charlene, John Conklin, me, Don Weiss, Tara, her twin Mara, Eleanor, Mike, Charlie Bravo, Charlie Delta, and Fred McCracken. Each of us has our own—well, we call them "quirks" to avoid the true nature of the fact that we're all certifiably insane—on some level—to do what we do as professionals.

We kill superheroes for a living.

I'm the normal one of the group, if we're being generous, because I'm here under false pretenses. I don't have "quirks" like these guys, but if you sit around and listen to them long enough, it's hard not to think that you might be one job away from tilting the pinball machine in your gray matter.

This is the Superhero Assassin Support Society (SASS for short—let it be known that I did *not* vote yes to that acronym), and I'm here because there's a traitor among us.

At least, an underground branch of the US government thinks so, and I'm getting paid to turn on my own kind...which leaves me wondering...which is worse, betraying your country, or betraying your friends?

The answer to that is pretty easy on a personal level, but, at the same time, if there's no honor among thieves, then there's certainly no honor among sassy people.

See what I did there?

***

The meeting went well, aside from every single lie Dallas told. Fred McCracken had a breakthrough and cried for the first time. Mike was the first to offer him a clean hanky, and those two have been rivals for thirty years in different aspects of their careers. Charlie Bravo and Charlie Delta didn't argue once over whom Mom loved best and John Conklin kept his hands where everyone could see them. All in all, I'd say it was a successful Tuesday, and I've only been attending for a month.

I'm now standing by the shoe counter waiting on

Jeff to bring me a pair of size elevens.

I don't know about actually bowling this time, because I'm nursing a wound in my side from the Patriotman gig. Let's just say that I had an *accident*, and for some reason, I'm not healing as fast as I normally do.

Charlene approaches with her handbag clutched to her chest like it's a shield—a zebra-striped shield with pink piping, but a shield nonetheless. She glances nervously from side to side, a tennis match of paranoid observation, and then manages to give me a smile.

"Hey, Leo," she says.

I have to be suspicious of everyone, because that's what I'm getting paid to do, but this is equally strange because she's never spoken a word to me outside of, "And how did that make you feel?"

Charlene has one thing in common with Dallas. She's not why I'm here either, and of that I'm positive.

Charlene is wearing a green shirt that complements her red hair, so I say, "If it isn't the Terror of Teal," and immediately question if I could've come up with a better line. She's a terror, all right. This five-eight bundle of cuteness is responsible for thirty-nine kills if you believe Homefront's data.

Every single superhero with the ability to look great in spandex has it out for her after CNC revealed her identity on *Tonight with Don Donner* a couple of weeks ago. It's no wonder the poor woman wears her suspicion like a heavy winter coat. I shake my head, embarrassed, and add, "Sorry, that was dumb."

Charlene titters nervously, like she wasn't sure she's supposed to laugh, and I feel a gooey warmth in my stomach. I can read people well enough to know that laughing when it's not warranted is a sign of liking someone—I mean *like* like—and I immediately feel as if I'm back in high school. Next thing you know, Charlene will be wearing my class ring, but it'll be too big for her and she'll have to wrap blue string around the band so it doesn't fall off her finger.

With that thought, my eyes go down to her hands, which I've never really examined before, and I see that they're large and sort of masculine. Maybe she wouldn't need the string after all, and—

She says, "I wanted to ask you something."

"Oh?"

Jeff shows up at the counter—stealthy bastard—and drops off the red, black, and gray size elevens. He sprays them with the anti-death-by-feet-fungus aerosol can and then seems to notice that Charlene and I are hanging out...together. He winks at me like she's not standing right there looking directly at him. I roll my eyes and take the fashionably awful shoes.

Charlene nods at a nearby table. "Want to go sit?"

"So it's a sit-down conversation, huh? Do I get detention afterward?" I shake my head, mentally punching myself in the nads because that was probably the lamest attempt at a witty flirtation that I've ever screwed up.

I've seriously been off my game since my divorce three years ago.

Thankfully, she doesn't notice, or doesn't care, because she titters again and heads to the table. The sound of bowling balls galloping down the lanes and the ear-shattering crash of flying pins reverberates around the room as we pull the seats out and sit across from each other. I feel like we should be cheek to cheek, sharing a root beer float.

Is it my imagination or is this absolutely awes—

See…this is the reason I haven't gotten remarried. A woman says hi to me, and I'm already planning who'll get the kids every other weekend.

Charlene lets go of her bag long enough to pull her seat closer to the table. An obnoxious funk emanates from the bowling shoes, and I discretely remove them from under my nose. They go into the chair beside me, but it's too late; the nostril damage has already been done.

"So," I say, "what's up?" My voice comes out

deeper than it usually is, and I can only assume that it was subconsciously intentional.

She says, "Can we talk about Dallas for a minute?"

I scoff and do that nasally snort of disapproval. "That woman. Jesus. I don't even have the words."

Charlene checks the surrounding area, and I follow her lead. Jeff remains behind the counter, spraying the fog of anti-death into a row of shoes while the other ten participants in SASS fling heavy balls at ten pieces of carved wood made from rock maple.

We don't really have a group leader, by the way. Too many strong-willed egos for that to happen, but if I had to pick someone to be in charge, I'd go with Charlene. While she may be more timid and paranoid than a mouse poking its head into a room filled with starving alley cats, she also seems levelheaded and is highly precise with a garrote wire, from the stories I've heard. But is that it? Are they just stories?

That's her trick, she says. Even superheroes need oxygen to survive, most of them anyway.

Charlene leans forward. Her lush red hair falls around her shoulders, and I get a whiff of perfume that smells like strawberry cream. She whispers, "It's none of my business, but how could you just sit there and let Dallas take credit for *your* work?"

Whoa. What?

TWO

One Month Earlier

I step off the commuter plane at PDX and feel the rush of cool rain and wind on my face. Portland's finest weather, and part of the reason I live here. I love that misty spritz.

The white-haired woman shuffling next to me says, "I thought it would be sunny."

"Vacation?" I ask.

"Visiting my sister. I hoped to get some sun and sand between my toes this close to the ocean."

I chuckle. She's clearly never been to the Pacific Northwest before, and I don't have the heart to tell her that the only waves she'll see in Portland are over in the Timbers' stadium.

The woman who had been sitting three rows up from me looks over her shoulder and smiles. Our eye contact lingers, and I'm already planning the honeymoon.

Forget it, bud. You promised yourself time to relax, remember?

Sometimes there are long weeks between jobs, and

honestly it's a good thing, because I don't care how much of a pro you are, you *need* time to wind down after eliminating someone that's universally beloved. It's a hard job, no matter how much some of them deserve it.

I like to sit on my front porch, with a blanket wrapped around my legs, watching the rain while I read non-fiction books about physics and marketing. I read the nerd journals to keep my mind sharp, but I'm also a businessman.

Do I question *why* I do this, why I fight for the wrong side? Sure. Every day. But, just as sure as somebody needs to dig ditches, somebody needs to do what I do.

Is there a wrong side? Depends on how you look at it.

We all have our faults. None of us are innocent. Even our heroes.

I've been at this for a few years now, but the worst was Polly Pettigrew, also known as White Cloud. She was originally the Blue Baroness, but she dropped out of the crime-fighting scene for a spell, and everyone thought she was dead. When she came back, she was essentially reborn, so the name change was appropriate. She was a billionaire heiress from somewhere deep in Texas—old money that came from centuries of her family controlling bountiful oil fields.

Polly was beautiful, and my God, did that woman have a heart of twenty-four carat gold when it came to the public persona. She was America's sweetheart on nightly television, but I'll tell you what, if you're cutting backroom deals with the Chinese over oil shipments to the tune of billions, Uncle Sam doesn't care how many little girls adore your action figure, you're taking a dirt nap.

Polly had a good soul, even if it was a little misguided, and my eight-year-old niece, Stephanie, absolutely worshipped her as White Cloud. Had to be done, though, because once you turn down a job, the men in the black suits who cut the checks may not come calling again.

So here I am, walking into the outer hub of PDX where they bring in all the small flights, stepping into the din of chatting travelers while they wait on their boarding instructions. I smell coffee and hamburgers, two of my favorite things in the world, next to a good northwest-brewed IPA, and immediately regret the half of a leftover peanut butter sandwich I had on the plane. What a waste of stomach space.

The woman I'm marrying in my mind glances back at me again and slows her marching speed.

Oh ho, what's this? Will we go to Belize or Hawaii?

She's wearing a charcoal gray blazer, matching gray slacks, and a white top. The carry-on suitcase she drags along is one of those standard black ones that everyone has, and I can see that it looks spotless. There are no scuffmarks or tears in the fabric. She doesn't have anything tied around the handle to indicate that it's hers, should she have to check it, and it also looks rather empty. It's not bulging like it's jammed with shoes, clothes, a hair dryer, and other necessities.

Either it's brand new, and she's here for a short stay, or that thing is a decoy. When you travel as much as I do, you get a certain sense for this stuff.

I get my answer right away when she says, "You look tired, Leo."

I sigh and nod. These approaches rarely surprise me anymore.

"Got a minute to talk?"

"Which agency?"

I ask this because the NSA pays the best, the CIA is finally learning that you have to open your wallet for quality work, and the FBI, well, let's just say that I have a certain appendage that could use servicing if they ever lowball me again.

"I doubt you've ever heard of us."

Interesting.

"Try me." I keep my eyes focused ahead, paying attention to the swarming, milling crowd. If there's one, there's another, and I like keeping these people on their toes. It's always more fun when I have them shaky and slightly less confident. I spot who I'm looking for about thirty feet ahead.

He's a dinosaur to be in this line of work and probably had his heyday when the Teletype was still in use. But, he's good at disguising himself because I never would've thought to check him until now. He got on the plane about twenty minutes after I did and I remember he bumped into me when he was trying to put his briefcase in the overhead compartment, then scrambled to get off the plane before everyone else. I see now that he was trying to get into position, but once I'm alone, I'll have to remember to check my collar and pockets for microscopic tracking devices in case he planted one.

"And," I add, "tell your buddy up there that if he wants to get someone's attention off him, he should start picking his nose. Works every time."

She smirks. "I'll be sure to let him know. Good eye, actually." As we pass the aging agent, she says, "Tough break, Agent Carter. Maybe next time."

Agent Carter's eyebrows arch high. He shakes his head, grumbles something unintelligible, then he tosses his newspaper into the trash. He follows, but not too closely.

The agent at my side clears her throat and says, "We realize you just got back from, you know, that job in Beijing, and Powder Keg was tougher than you—"

I hold my palm up to her. "Nope."

"Nope what?"

"He *wasn't* tougher than I expected and not another word until, one, you tell me how you know where I've been, and two, you tell me which agency because I don't make a habit of talking to people I've just met. Stranger danger."

This elicits a throaty laugh from her. Did I say something funny?

"We know more about you than your own mother, Leo, but I appreciate your candor."

No, she doesn't...she does *not* know the truth. But, I play along. "Then you're aware that I'm not a fan of secrecy."

"You like northwest IPAs with a low IBU, right? Let me buy you one. I know a good spot."

Okay, now I'm impressed. "Local brew?"

"Wouldn't have it any other way."

***

I never accept rides from ultra-secretive government agents, especially ones who refuse to identify themselves until they have a cold brew in their hand.

However, her invitation intrigued me because the way this *usually* goes is via a self-destructing cell phone that receives vague texts, handed to me by some "whitebread" dude in dark glasses. Good thing I operate well on little instruction.

She doesn't even tell me her name until the waitress brings two heavy mugs full of a golden amber liquid. These things are made of such thick glass, you could use them as hammers.

She says, "Wait until you taste this. New guys in town doing some amazing craft work."

"How do you know I haven't had it before?" I ask. She'd ordered them while I was in the restroom. I couldn't find any tracking devices, but if they think they already know so much about me, I doubt it matters.

She grins and sips her beer. "Please. You know the answer to that."

I shrug and let her have this small win. Chess matches can take a long time.

The IPA is amazing, unlike any I've ever tasted, and I have to work to contain my excitement. She's right, the bitter taste of IPA is almost negligible and there's this sort of heady, fruit-forward taste with a soft touch on the back end. Magnificent. I smack my lips and feel a grin stretch to my ears.

"See?"

I lick the foam off my upper lip and take another swig. "That's just…unbelievable. So good. I can't decide if I should propose to you or threaten to walk if you don't tell me what I want to know."

Her eyes soften over the rim of her mug. When she sets it down, I notice the small trace of lipstick left behind on the glass. "Let's start with the latter."

I inspect the bar. We're alone except for the bored bartender and the waitress folding napkins around silverware. The sounds of basketball, scuffling shoes and bouncing rubber, along with the voice of an excited sportscaster, emanate from the embedded speakers while Agent Carter sits at the bar, arms crossed, watching the Blazers play. They're winning, finally.

"Great," I say. "Who the fuck are you?" I force a smile to look real, but she can sense my impatience. Time for the game to be over. I'm walking in dangerous territory here and I've let it go too long already.

"Agent Lisa Kelly," she answers. "Sorry about the

discretion. Can't be too careful in airports. Too many cameras, too many ears."

"And you're with…whom? You're too laid back for a spook. You're drinking a beer so you can't be one of those stiffs from the FBI, and the NSA would do a handoff in the grocery store. So that leaves, what? Secret Service? Homefront?"

"What if I told you that we're so far off the books, the president doesn't even know about us?"

"Then I'd call bullshit and walk out the door. I might finish my beer first, but that'd be about the end of our conversation."

Agent Kelly leans back in her seat and sips. She has green eyes, unnaturally tan skin for someone who likely spends more time working than enjoying her days off, and brunette hair pulled into a tight bun. I've been *seeing* her face, but this is the first time I've actually *looked* at her. She's a beautiful woman. I'd put her at about forty, close to my age, but not a day over.

She stares at me intently while I wait. It doesn't take long before I grow uncomfortable and say, "What?"

"I'm waiting on you to walk."

So she's really going to play it out, huh? Might as well see how far she'll take it.

"All right." I lift my shoulders and let them drop with a huff. "Let's hear it."

"Thought so. They said you were the curious type."

"They who?"

"The data nerds."

"And exactly where does this data come from?"

"Around."

I look at my watch. I don't really care what time it is, but this is getting old.

"Somewhere to be?"

"Oh my God." She's maddening. "Are you married?"

"No, why do you ask?"

"I'm not surp—never mind."

Agent Kelly chuckles and signals for the waitress to bring us another round. "Deke…Agent Carter over there, he and I are from DPS."

I'd never heard of it before and tell her so. I also don't call bullshit, nor do I get up and walk out the door. She has my attention. There isn't much I don't know about the darker side of our fine governmental establishment.

"Direct Protection Services," she continues. "When the suits see certain patterns in your testing, you're given the option to take a post with DPS. It's almost like the Witness Protection Program, in a way, except for the fact that we're not running from anyone. If you join DPS, you say your goodbyes and then you vanish. All records, all traces…"—she swipes her hand across the table—"gone. You never existed. From then on, it's service until you retire or take the long road home."

"All in the name of God and country? Admirable, I suppose."

Agent Kelly impatiently glances around for the waitress. "Sacrifices were made, but the pay makes it worth it."

"Wild guess says that Lisa Kelly isn't your real name."

She shakes her head. "Just like Leo Craft isn't yours."

"Touché, but that one's free." Something occurs to me—the way she fidgets in her seat, the way she slyly glances at Deke Carter for approval, and how her fingers can't stop fiddling with a packet of sugar; they're all signs of some underlying current of insecurity. "You're new at this, aren't you? At least with the DPS."

"What makes you say that?"

The hint of surprise on her face is all I need to see. It means she can be manipulated if the situation calls for it. Somebody thought she was prepared for this role, but you can't make up for inherent human nature. "What do you need from me, Agent Kelly?"

When she gives an indirect answer, for once, I'm not prepared for what I hear.

THREE

Present Day

There are a few cardinal rules you don't break in this business. The first is don't trust anyone. You start making friends, having drinks, watching the game together, it's easy to slip into this comfortable place where you share tips and tricks and the next thing you know, some muscled prick in red tights with flames down the side is knocking at your front door because your "friend" didn't live up to that supposed role.

Happened once, never again.

The second rule is, nobody will ever understand why you do what you do, so don't bother trying to explain it to them. I say this because I've gotten close—I mean like, *close*—to a couple of women who could've been The One, since my divorce, and I thought they would get it. I thought they would get *me*. Nope. They beat feet down the front path fast enough to leave a cloud of dust in their wake.

Happened twice, never again.

I don't like moving halfway across the country to hide, and I don't like having my heart broken.

I guess there's an unofficial addendum to rule

number two; don't fall in love in the first place.

I'd like to again, believe me, but there's no room for it. Well, I shouldn't say that. I do it all the time in my imagination. I just don't act on it.

The third rule, and quite possibly the most important, is never, ever get lazy. All it takes is one mistake, one tiny little hiccup, and you're exposed. You're wide open and you might as well draw a bulls-eye on your back.

I broke rule number three. I don't know how or when, but the fact that Charlene sits across from me, smelling like delicious, creamy strawberries, waiting on an answer, means that I slipped up.

I stare at her with abject speechlessness and race through detail after detail in my mind. I'm clean, I know I am. I can't think of a single thing I might have screwed up with the Patriotman job. I didn't so much as leave a flake of skin behind. There was no way in hell that I—

"Leo?" Charlene butts in.

"What? Oh, right? What was the question?" I know damn well what the question was but I need two more seconds to think.

Jeff drops off a basket of fries and says, "On the house, lovebirds."

Really? Really, Jeff? Do I need that right now?

"You're better than that, you're better than Dallas, and I'm half-tempted to march over there and tell Kim Jong Un where she can shove it."

"She's from *South* Korea."

Charlene looks up at the ceiling—as if she's addressing God—as if she's asking "Why me?"

My inability to focus on the imperative element must get under her skin. For the first time ever, she lets go of the zebra-bag shield long enough to hold her hands out to me. She pleads angrily, "You can't let her get away with it."

"It pisses me off too, but why does it matter?" This question is about as close to an admission of responsibility as I can get. By acknowledging the fact that Dallas stole my thunder isn't cool, I'm opening the door just a crack to let Charlene know that she's right. I don't want to do it, but man, I'm stumped. If she knows, she knows.

"It's not right, that's all."

"Charlene?"

"What?"

"What's the real reason?"

Charlene glances over her shoulder. The other ten members of SASS are down at the lanes, arguing over whether Tara (or maybe it's Mara) stepped over the line. Charlie Delta is so red in the face, I think I can see a vein bulging from here.

Dallas cackles with laughter.

Charlene turns back to me with a scrunched up nose, almost like she's snarling, and says, "Because she's a no-talent ass clown, and you're one of the best in the business. I can't stand the fact that she's got all those other schmucks wrapped around her little finger, and they worship her like she's some kind of…"

"Superhero?" It's hard to ignore the irony.

"Whatever. If I didn't think she would run and snitch on me to the suits running DPS, I'd expose every dirty little secret she has."

My hand goes up in the air, and I unintentionally use a ketchup-coated French fry to accentuate my surprise. It wobbles limply between my thumb and forefinger when I say, "Hang on, *what* did you say?"

"That I'd love to expose every little—"

"No, the part about DPS. You're talking about *the* DPS?" I've been working with Agents Lisa Kelly and Deke Carter for about four weeks. I thought they were invisible…to everybody.

Charlene snatches up her handbag again and resumes using it as a protective shield. She tries to backpedal. "I-I-I didn't say anything about—you have ketchup running down your fingers."

Indeed I do, but more important things are hanging out there like the most pregnant *oops* in the history of mankind. "You said DPS, Charlene. Direct Protection Services?"

Only when she nods do I finally drop the fry and wipe the ketchup off my hand.

"Who's your handler there? And is that how you know about my work in the Maldives?"

Charlene shrugs. I've quickly gone from lovesick teenager to highly paranoid, distrustful, elite superhero assassin Leo Craft. It's amazing how three little letters can change an entire scenario.

I repeat, "How do you know about DPS?" While I wait on her to make up her mind about answering, I breathe deeply, cycling through my options. Not one of them is good. They all lead to a fade-to-black that I don't enjoy.

Charlene's hand snaps out to grab a fry and draws it back in. She nibbles on the crusty end and says, "I'm getting soft."

That tender spot for her winks to life again like a distant star poking through the darkness. It takes a lot to admit that, especially among the ego-driven culture we inhabit. I feel the muscles in my face relax. My leg stops jackhammering the floor, and I lean up onto the table with my elbows. "I can see why. That *Don Donner* thing must be tough."

Charlene points her chin at the lanes. The arguments are over, and the thunderous bowling has resumed. "It's because of her."

"Dallas?"

"When DPS dropped her and took me on, she flipped out."

"Hold up. Dallas worked for DPS, too?"

"Yeah. And she's the one that revealed my identity to CNC and Don Donner."

"Are you absolutely *positive*?" I ask, but I already know the answer. If Charlene knew this to be true, Dallas would've been dead already.

"It *has* to be her. And now that I've fucked this up," she says, pointing at me, then her chest, "I could use your help."

And the truth comes out. That's why Charlene is *really* upset—and good Lord, who wouldn't be—with Dallas, as long as she's the real snitch, and now that I've had a second to process, I'm starting to think that Charlene's little "uh-oh" wasn't so accidental at all. She doesn't give a crap about Dallas stealing my glory, she just wants to watch her burn. Plus, if she's working for DPS, then it's easy to see how she could've potentially learned that the Patriotman job was mine, but there are some seriously gaping leaks if that level of interdepartmental sharing is going on. I'll need to have a discussion with Kelly and Carter as soon as possible. Who knows what other details about me are floating around out there?

This is not good.

This is not good *at all*.

But it's *Charlene*, though. If there's one person in this group who I would be slightly okay with knowing what's happening on the back end, it would be her, but damn, it's dangerously close to breaking Rule Number One.

Yet again, I repeat another question from earlier. "Who's your handler?"

"Two of them, actually. Crenshaw and Hawthorne. You know them?"

"No, just my two. Carter and Kelly. Kelly's lead and Carter…well, I don't know what he does other than sit around and look pissed that I made him the first time we met."

"Older guy? Should've hung the gloves up thirty years ago?"

"Yeah."

"He's a teddy bear if he likes you."

This doesn't surprise me. I'd bet that Charlene captivates most men. And I say this without the slightest hint of sexism or chauvinism, but that's probably how she got in so close to all the men in tights that she's eliminated. If everyone in the group is telling the truth about their number of recorded kills, then Charlene is first, I'm second, Tara and Mara are third, and so on and so forth. I consider myself top-notch in the skill department, but Charlene, she's something else.

Back before Charlene became the nearly incapacitated paranoid recluse that she is now, if she approached me in a bar wearing a cocktail dress and a smile, and had murder on her mind, I'd be clawing at a garrote wire around my neck before the end of the night. So they say. As the story goes. Blah blah blah.

She adds, "Deke's the one that told me about the Maldives."

"Figures." I nibble on another fry, trying to gauge her facial expressions, wondering what's actually going on here. Study people long enough, you can pick up on all these little micro-movements that will tell you more about them than an all-access autobiography. A twitch at the corner of an eye, a wrinkled nose, a smile ever-so-slightly dipping into less of a smile…they all tell you so much.

If I'm reading her right, so far this is legit.

"Why'd he tell *you* about that?"

"He's not your biggest fan."

There it is. There's what I'm looking for: briefly, it's that almost imperceptible flinch of the fatty skin tissue residing above her cheekbones, or, in layman's terms, a squint. It's a microscopic hint that she's focusing on what she's trying to say to me, as if she's forcing it to sound true and get past my defenses.

It could be innocent. It could be the dust particles flying around in here because I can feel the air of the ventilation system gently puffing against the back of my neck.

Maybe, but I don't think so.

What she's saying isn't quite true because, while Deke Carter *isn't* my biggest fan, I can tell that I'm growing on him, and I doubt he'd betray my cover.

Charlene, Charlene, Charlene…what are you up to?

I haven't survived this long by being an ignorant fool. It's not time to start now. I have to remember, absolutely *have* to accept the fact that this woman is a highly trained assassin. Paranoid or not, if we're on opposing sides of something I'm not familiar with, I can't risk allowing the walls around me to fall.

Do I test her now? Do I play along until I see what she's up to? Should I punt and hope to stay in the game for a while longer?

An incomprehensible thought occurs to me, and

Jesus, it would be one risky but amazing long con if that's what she's going for: what if her debilitating paranoia is just a charade? What if she, or someone at DPS, intentionally leaked her identity to Don Donner and CNC to set up this elaborate plot to draw me into a trap?

Call it prophetic, call it suspicious, but plotting out scenarios like this in my head is what's keeping me alive.

Would she risk her life that way? Every superhero in the world is gunning for her right now. Am I worth that?

What did *I* do? Why would they be after *me*?

Yeah, punting is the safest option. For now.

Maybe I'm totally going down the path of insanity here, becoming truly, amazingly mistrustful like Charlene, and maybe that subconscious blip of wrongdoing on her face was nothing more than a speck of dust in her eye, but better safe than dead.

It occurs to me that it was awfully strange how a government organization that I've never heard of pops up out of the darkest depths of national secrecy to recruit me. I need to step away from this for a while. I need to go talk to my contact that knows the answer to more questions than a *Jeopardy!* champion.

We call him the Oracle, like that lady in The

Matrix, but really he's a retired CIA guy named Phil that has more connections than there are grains of sand on the beach. If Phil doesn't know about the DPS, then I have plenty of reason to worry.

How do I make a fast exit without alerting Charlene that I'm onto her?

Thank God, it couldn't have been better timing: my phone buzzes in my pocket. "Hang on, Char," I say, holding up a finger, "let me check this." The ID screen tells me it's Agent Kelly. I apologize to Charlene and tell her that I need to take it, that it could be important. "Can we talk later?"

She looks let down. Is it genuine? I'm so flustered that I can't read her right now. "I guess so. Don't forget me, though. I still need your help with Dallas." She meekly pulls her handbag close to her chest and turns away.

I'm hustling out the door when I hear John Conklin shout, "Fall you bastards, fall!"

Among all this craziness, I'm kinda hoping he just rolled his first perfect game.

FOUR

Three Weeks Earlier

I'm sitting on my front porch enjoying some well-earned downtime when a black sedan with non-descript government plates parks in front of my house. I sit up and throw the blanket off my legs, then set the latest masterpiece about particle physics to the side. I don't understand a word of it, but it makes for interesting reading.

Whoever is parked in the sedan shouldn't be here. Most of the major agencies know that I don't operate on such a familiar level. My *house*? No way that the NSA, CIA, or even those trundling knuckle-draggers over at the FBI would risk blowing my identity by showing up on my doorstep. They know better.

It sits there quietly with the engine running. The windows are tinted, and I can't see inside. I'm tempted to get up and take a stroll down the front walk, but from where I'm sitting, my guns and poisons and *nun chucks* and swords are a helluva lot closer. For probably the first time ever, I slacked off and didn't bring a weapon outside with me; I regret the oversight.

Who in the hell is that?

Local law enforcement doesn't know about my degree of involvement with the United States government, or most of the governments of NATO for that matter, so if it's a couple of departmental detectives here to brace me about something, then it has nothing to do with my black-ops, off-paper work.

Finally, the engine shuts off. I scoot up to the edge of my seat, butt cheeks right on the lip of the rocking chair, with my toes pointed toward the front door, ready to dart inside. I don't normally get antsy, but this is highly out of character for anyone I might be in contact with at the national government level.

Both doors open simultaneously, and I flinch, waiting, holding my breath, until out climb Agents Kelly and Carter. I exhale heavily and mutter, "Unbelievable." I stand up and walk to the top step, folding my arms across my chest, glaring them down with a stare of disapproval as they make their way up to the house.

Agent Kelly is all smiles. Deke Carter stares at me like I'm the guy who stole his daughter's virginity on prom night. Kelly says, "Good to see you again, Leo." Deke grunts and turns his attention down the street.

"The hell are you doing here at my house?"

"In the neighborhood. Thought we might stop by, see how you were doing."

"In the neighborhood. Right." I grind my teeth and lower my voice. "Are you insane? Broad daylight? What's wrong with a phone call?"

"We could've, but this stuff is always better done in person. Less breadcrumbs that way. Eyes, ears everywhere."

I glance nervously around at the nearby houses. It's nine a.m. on a Wednesday morning, so most everyone is at work. The Marshalls across the street are on vacation, and Bill Tuttle, who lives next door, is retired and, fortunately, deaf and blind. His daughter Mindy won't be by for another couple of hours to check up on him.

Flinging a pointed finger at my front door, I order them to get inside.

Agent Kelly's smile stays plastered to her face—she's enjoying my agitation—and Deke Carter does nothing more than lift his chin at me as he passes. One last look around to make sure nobody saw, and I step in behind them.

Agent Kelly whistles. "Nice place, Leo. That's a real Picasso, isn't it?"

"It's a print," I lie. "Ten bucks at a yard sale." Truth is, that thing set me back like four million. It's a little known piece from his blue period, and I got it off this billionaire the last time I was in Madrid. Taking

SUPER

out the superhero known as *El Jefe* had proved to be more difficult than the Spanish government had expected, so I had charged them double, and the Picasso piece was my own personal reward for a job well done.

"And look at this couch," she says, running her hands across the plush black leather. "You could melt into it."

"Sit down if you want. Deke, you can, too."

He grunts and says, "Coffee?" with an expectant look. I should be offended, but this is the first word I've ever heard him speak, so I let it slide.

"Lisa?" I drop the formality with her. Might as well, since she's inside my freaking house.

"I'll have one, too. Thanks."

She looks good today, wearing a dark blue suit with a cream top and matching heels. Nice touch. Her hair is down, and even though it looks great, I preferred it up, like the way she wore it on the day we met.

They sit while I head into the kitchen. I shuffle through the cabinets, acting like I'm getting prepped to make their coffee, when what I'm really doing is trying to remember where I put that Smith & Wesson snub-nosed .38; was it in the junk drawer or where I keep the knives or—there it is, in the drawer with the cooking utensils, because that makes perfect sense, right? Why *wouldn't* it be there? I tuck it into my waistband at my back and cover it with the hem of my long-sleeve t-shirt, then set about brewing the coffee.

As it gurgles and steams into the pot, I walk back into the living room. I lean up against the doorjamb to give myself easy access to the .38 if I need it.

Lisa and Deke both have to turn their heads to the side to see me. She smiles and says, "Come sit down." She points to the matching armchair on the opposite side. I sleep there more often than I do in my own king-sized bed. That chair, I swear, is like dozing on a bed of fluffy white clouds.

"I'll stand," I say. "Gotta wait on the coffee."

"You don't need the gun, Leo." Lisa winks. It's still not a measure of reassurance that I'm comfortable with.

I don't question how she suspects it's there because it's fairly obvious. She's been trained to know her shit and to anticipate stuff like this long before it's necessary. Given that, I respect her skill and move over to the armchair, but I don't sit back, nor do I relax. The cool metal of the handgun presses into my skin, and I've practiced this scenario enough to know that it can be in my hand and aimed in four-tenths of a second.

I would've done well in the Old West.

"So," Lisa says, scooting up to the edge of the couch, or trying to, anyway. It's deep and so thick that she literally has to squirm to adjust her position. Deke doesn't bother. He appears disinterested in me and keeps his eyes trained on my Picasso. I suppose he's pretending to study it, but in reality, he's monitoring me from his peripheral vision. "Nice place you got here."

"Seriously?"

"What?"

"Cut the bull—*why* are you here, in my home? You only told me about the Sassy Club or whatever the hell it is last week. I went on Tuesday and Thursday and you need to back the hell off. You don't find a traitor in a week, and let me tell you something else—those people are insane."

Her smile fades like she's disappointed. I couldn't care less. She says, "I can see that we've put you out a bit, so I'll just get right to the point. We've discussed your current status with your handlers among the other agencies, and everyone feels that it's best for you to come work solely with us until this situation is resolved."

"Bullshit." There's no way that she got clearance from Eric Landers, Joe Gaylord, or Conner Carson all at the same time. It's likely that they're familiar with each other on a professional level, based on the fact that they're all working for the sake of national interests, but I doubt that they know that each of the others works with me on an individual basis. I don't care how convincing Lisa is. I flat-out refuse to believe that all three of them would simultaneously agree to give up such an asset, and I say that without a hint of bruised ego.

Plus, I have such clandestine relations with these men that I find it impossible to believe that she and Deke would be able to make the connections.

A sly smile creeps back across her lips. "Eric, Joe, and Conner—all three of them—were very understanding when we suggested that your services were better used elsewhere."

Well, there you have it. Call me flabbergasted. Maybe the DPS has more pull than I thought. I'd checked around with a few of my contacts to see if any of them had ever heard of Direct Protection Services, but no dice. That hadn't surprised me considering the fact that I was unaware of their existence as well. I hadn't made an attempt with the Three Amigos either because, for one thing, I didn't want them to *know* that I was ignorant of something since that might allow them to feel like they had the slightest upper hand.

For another thing, while I was pondering asking, I had been concerned that if they weren't familiar with DPS, then what kind of shitstorm would it set off among them if a fourth agency—one previously unknown—was snooping around, looking to steal my in-demand services? In the end, I left it alone, figuring I could always meddle around later.

I clear my throat and hear the end of the brew cycle beeping in the kitchen. "Coffee's ready," I say, standing, walking away. I use it as an excuse to clear my head for a second. I pour three cups and debate on adding a little something extra to theirs. "Cream or sugar?" I call into the living room.

Or cyanide, perhaps? The vial is right there in the drawer.

"Both for me," Lisa answers. "Deke says neither."

"Coming right up." A thought I have makes me curious, because what she's telling me now doesn't quite jibe with what she said last week. I step gently back into the living room, holding the coffees delicately to prevent any of the scalding liquid from sloshing out, and for a moment, I consider throwing both cups in their faces and making a break for it.

But, I don't, because if they have connections with my three handlers, and are able to sway their opinions, then it would most likely be the end of my career. No more offing dudes and ladies in multi-colored tights for me.

"Coffee for you, ma'am. And Deke, this ought to put some hair on your chest. You look like you could use a few more." Deke lifts one corner of his mouth in the slightest grin. Maybe he's warming up to me. As they both take hesitant sips, testing the temperature, I back up to my cushy chair and ease down. "I'm curious about something."

Lisa lifts her eyebrows at me in response.

"You said last week that you were so off the books that even the President doesn't know about DPS. How'd you pull rank on the NSA, the CIA, and the FBI without clueing them in?"

Lisa sets her coffee mug down—on a coaster, thank God—and says, "Give us a little credit, Leo. We weren't born yesterday."

"You maybe. Deke here looks like he might've fought a stegosaurus for scraps."

That comment results in a hearty chuckle from Deke. Not that I'm warming up to *him*, but obviously the man appreciates a witty sense of humor.

Lisa continues, "Your three contacts think we're with the Secret Service, and they don't need to know any different. Is that understood?" The hopeful look on her face suggests that I should nod to let her know I got the hint.

I do just that, but then I add, "Secret Service? What kind of pitch did you run with? Those sunglass-wearing mutes have nothing to do with double agents, do they?"

"Deke had the idea that we would approach it as if we had intelligence indicating President Palmer's life had been threatened by an extremist group of superheroes, and who better to help protect the C.I.C. than the guy responsible for taking out those exact same people?"

Deke curses when he spills coffee on his stark white shirt. I've heard him use two words now, and the second shouldn't be repeated in polite company.

"Rags are in the kitchen, Deke. Second drawer down below the coffee. Ignore the .45 if it's still in there."

He nods and toddles into the other room, swiping at his tie.

I say to Lisa, "Let me get this straight. You told three of the most powerful law enforcement agencies in the US that a super*hero* was planning an assassination attempt? Look, I may just be an ant on the bottom of the food chain, but that sounds like the dumbest idea I've ever heard. No offense to Deke, because hey, seems like it worked, but why in the world didn't you go with a super*villain* instead? I heard the Black Viper was working on something big. Starbeast is back. FireShot, King Killer, Dr. Craze? Any of those guys would be perfect culprits, but now, you've probably got entire task forces out there chasing down a threat that doesn't exist. And if distraction is your plan, so be it, but damn if that's not reckless endangerment when you're causing valuable resources to be allocated to chasing ghosts."

Lisa nods throughout my speech. When I finish, she looks underneath the coffee table at my feet and then glances around the floor like she's searching for something.

"What're you doing?"

"Trying to see where you keep the soapbox."

"Very funny."

"Here's the thing, Leo… You're right. We could've done that. We could've given them a spiel about how the craziest masterminds in history were cooking up a credible threat against the president, but there's no way in hell that Eric, Joe, and Conner would've handed you over for that. They would've laughed in our faces. They would've told us to suck it up and find someone that worked on that side of things. But, and this was the integral part, who better to chase down disgruntled superheroes than the guy who's been eliminating them for the past three years?"

Okay, she has a point. I tell her as much, and she shrugs off my approval as Deke re-enters the living room. "And you came here just to tell me that officially I work for you guys now?"

"Yeah. And don't worry, you're still on the support group thing, but we've got a little side project for you."

"Like what?"

"Ever been to the Maldives?"

FIVE

Present Day

I had ignored Agent Kelly's call, and she didn't leave a message, so now I'm standing here on the street corner wondering what she wanted. Knowing that the SASS meeting had ended, she was probably calling for a status update, but she usually waits until the next morning. Maybe she's getting antsy. It's been a month, and I'm no closer to finding her traitor.

That can wait until tomorrow. I have more important things on my mind.

The Oracle, or Phil, as he actually prefers, lives in a modest two-story condo in the Northwest District in Portland. It's within walking distance of a number of awesome shops, pubs, and more coffee joints than anyone would ever need. There's a bagel place, too, that will knock your socks off if you're wearing any with your Birkenstocks. (Don't Birkenstocks come furnished with socks? Just asking.)

I climb up his steps, checking the tree-lined street both north and south to see if I have a tail. The only thing that might be out of place is a gas-guzzling Hummer parked two blocks up, which is astronomically out of sorts for how green this city prides itself to be. It's a little past ten p.m. and the soft glow of the street lamps don't help much, but if I focus just the right way, I can tell that it has a California license plate.

Tourists.

There's a hostel around the corner, but I'm thinking if you can afford the gas and car payments for a monstrosity like that, you can afford a hotel downtown, something swanky like The Nines.

Is it out of place enough to worry? I doubt it, but it wouldn't surprise me if some hipster decides to key the thing in the middle of the night. Can't say I would blame them.

Phil's place hasn't changed in the last decade. I recruited him for backup info gathering when I got into this business. Aside from the members of SASS, my handlers, my mom, and the two ex-girlfriends I stupidly opened my mouth to, Phil is the only person who is aware of what I do for a living.

He gets paid handsomely to keep quiet about it.

If I were to trust someone implicitly, Phil would be on the top of the list, probably more than Dear Old Mom. She's not happy with my chosen profession, and I wouldn't put it past her to leak my identity to *Tonight with Don Donner* just to get me to retire.

I knock on his front door. Even in the low light, I can tell that the black paint is fading. I wait impatiently, so long that I'm ready to knock again before I spot the subtle swish of a curtain falling back into place.

There goes the metallic clunk of the deadbolt, followed by the jangling chain, and then the latch on the knob.

He opens the front door—crazy bed hair standing at attention on the top of his head—wearing a red flannel bathrobe and matching slippers. Underneath that, he's got on purple silk pajamas. He doesn't offer a greeting. He simply stands there looking annoyed.

I say, "You look like the Oregonian version of Hugh Hefner."

Phil smirks. "If only."

"How're you doing, Dad?"

"It's late, Leo."

"You got anything better to do?"

"Sleep, for one thing. Get in here before somebody spots you."

I check the street and sidewalk one last time, and step inside, satisfied that I wasn't followed by Charlene or anyone else.

Dad. Phil.

Phil. Dad.

Bio Dad, a man named Martin Lauderhill, walked

out on Mom when I was two, and we never heard from him again. My connections say he died in the early '90s from a heroin overdose. Whatever.

Thirty-five years later, I still waffle on what to call Phil. He insists on "Phil," but he's been in my life since I was four years old. He's my dad, plain and simple. Being the manly men we are, beating our chests and chasing down mastodons with sticks, we've never really discussed this conundrum. I mean, gauging by the way he constantly reminds me to call him by his proper name, I'd say he has attachment issues, but it's been a game we've played for almost four decades. If it *is* an attachment thing, then it's likely due to his years and years of undercover work for the CIA.

Phil was a Cold War spy, and a damn good one, too, so it's easy to see how he wouldn't want to get emotionally involved with anything. It's not a huge stretch to see why he and Mom divorced. Well, that and his Russian mistress, Ilya, might've had something to do with it.

He called me "Son" once and refuses to acknowledge it whenever I bring it up.

Phil moves a stack of newspapers and a crocheted blanket off his decrepit couch and motions for me to sit down. He asks me if I want coffee.

"Got anything stronger?"

"It's gonna be one of those conversations, is it?"

"Yup. 'Fraid so."

He waddles over to the mini-bar that I installed for him two years ago—a Christmas gift that actually put a real smile on the man's face—and pours us both a hearty helping of Glenfiddich twenty-year-old scotch that he keeps around for emergencies. I notice that he's gained some weight since Ilya left him. And by "left him," I mean, "went to Heaven" six months ago.

Mom even came to the funeral. That took a lot of willpower and heart, but as insane as it sounds, she and Ilya had become acquaintances, often sharing war stories about Phil. Their mutual annoyances had served as plenty of laughter over wine. Phil has asked Mom if she'd like another go at it, and the last I'd heard, she's considering the possibility.

Why? God knows. Forgiven but not forgotten? Could be all the money he has and refuses to spend.

Phil apologizes for the lack of ice and hands me the tumbler. "You shouldn't ruin good scotch like that anyway."

I don't feel like arguing with him. If it enhances the flavor in different ways then—never mind. I nod and down it in one gulp. Yeah, it's that kinda night.

He looks at me like I kicked a puppy. "Jesus, you shouldn't waste it like that either. Take your time, enjoy it. Things that bad?"

Oh God, the burn. I cough and beat on my chest. "I'm in something deep, Dad, and I don't know what's going on."

"*Phil.*"

I roll my eyes. "Can we not do that right now? This is serious."

"Yeah, yeah. So what's going on?"

"You've been watching the news lately, haven't you? Seen the Patriotman thing?"

"God, how could I not? They interrupted *Wheel of Fortune* the other night, again, just to say they'd found another new lead—wait. Why do you ask?" He leans forward in his armchair, cradling the tumbler in his hands. They shake a little, but they always do that. You couldn't unnerve the man if you told him there was a ticking bomb under his seat.

I flatten my lips against each other, frown, and raise my hand.

His surprise is evident. "That was *you?*"

For the past three years, Phil has been a part of nearly every mission I've ever worked. He's a master at digging up details on people—their strengths, weaknesses, and habits—superheroes in particular, and

ERNIE LINDSEY

he's one of the reasons I've been so successful. I never mentioned the Patriotman gig to him because it was too big, too…*wrong*, and I didn't want him to think less of me.

I had ruined the hopes and dreams of so many little boys and girls. Crime rates the world over were already rising. North Korea, just this morning, had announced the reboot of their nuclear weapons testing program.

And it was all because of my handiwork.

"Oh, God, Leo, that's over the line. You were…what were you thinking, son?"

He calls me *son*. That's how much it affects him. "I know, Phil. Lecture me later, but right now, I need information before—this is so deep, I honestly don't even know what I'm involved in. I guess the worst that could happen is being six feet under, but—"

"Wrong, bud."

"Wrong?"

"The worst thing that can happen is somebody turns you over to SALCON."

SALCON is sort of like the NATO of superheroes.

Superhero Alliance of Cooperative Nations.

Trips off the tongue when you say it, which is why SALCON is much easier.

It's made up of representatives from around the world and though they publicly deny it—while those of us behind the scenes know the truth—they've been accused of prisoner detainment and torture that violates all sorts of international treaties. It's whispered that they're worse than most supervillains.

What does it say about your character if you do bad things while claiming it's all in the name of good?

I suppose I should ask myself the same question.

"And in your position," Phil continues, "if they ever found out what you've been up to for the last three years, it'd be a helluva lot worse than a dirty cop going to prison. You'd never see sunlight again, Leo, and that'd be the easy part."

"The people they have on the case are morons. They'll never get within ten miles of me, but they're not the ones I have to worry about. The only way SALCON finds out is if I tell them myself, or—" For a moment, I had forgotten about Charlene. "I, uh, it's more complicated…"

"How many people, Leo?"

I shake my head softly. "That's the thing; I don't know."

Phil lowers his eyes and stares into his scotch like he's reading tea leaves, looking for an answer. He takes a deep breath, huffs, and then downs his glass in a single gulp as well. Without a word, he gets up and walks over to the bar, then grabs the Glen by the bottle's neck and pours me another one before he sits down. I fight the urge to blather everything I've done, know, and seen over the past month, but Phil is a master of extracting information. He'll ask me the right questions.

This particular skill set of his is the reason I never got away with anything while I was in high school.

Phil sips again, smacks his lips—a habit I picked up, apparently—and asks again, "How many?"

"My two handlers," I say, counting them off finger by finger. "Another S.A. named Charlene, possibly *her* handlers, their supervisors, and…" And God, I hate to admit this, but I add, "Possibly another S.A. named Dallas."

He doesn't get angry. He simply shakes his head, disappointed. "Goddamn it, Leo. That's a fucking football team. What were you thinking?"

"It wasn't my—"

"Fault, I know. It never was, never is." Phil reclines in his chair and rubs his hands through his hair. "Explain to me how two other S.A.'s know about it. Let's start there."

I realize I should start back at the beginning, back when Agent Kelly and Deke Carter stepped up to me in PDX, but I know Phil well enough to realize that not answering what he's asking will lead to a round-and-round that I don't want to deal with.

You know what? The hell with it. We'll waste too much time dancing around details if we attack the timeline like a Tarantino movie.

"That's the middle of the story, Dad. I need to go back further than that."

"*Phil.*"

"Fine, *Phil*. So about a month ago, I land in PDX after that last gig with the...you remember..."

"Yeah, the guy. Right, right."

"I get the *hi-how-are-ya* from two D.C. suits right there in the terminal. Didn't surprise me because I'm used to approaches like that, you know? Just not in plain sight in the airport."

"Brazen bastards, huh? Greenhorns?"

"Nah. Deke Carter? He's old enough that you should know him."

"Deke Carter... Nope, no clue."

Strange. I thought Dad knew all those Cold War dudes.

"The other one is Lisa Kelly. Close to my age. Not too much of a hard-ass, but she's sharp. Good back and forth. Pretty, too."

"And that matters...why?"

"Doesn't. It's a detail."

He looks at me sideways. "Mmm-hmm. What'd they want?"

"Said they had some work for me, on the good side of things. They're from DPS, which I'd never heard of."

Phil raises an eyebrow.

"Direct Protection Services?"

I realize I'm in deep shit when he says, "Who are they?"

Six

Three Weeks Earlier, Con't.

I'm riding in the back of the black sedan with tinted windows. This is highly unconventional because I was informed that I wouldn't be able to bring a weapon to protect myself, nor would I be allowed to see where we were going once we got to a certain point on I-5, north toward Seattle. Back at my house, I'd insisted that if I were going to do what they were asking, I would need to talk to someone higher up the food chain than Agent Lisa Kelly and Deke Carter.

She made some phone calls and got approval, so now I'm sitting here with my arms crossed over my chest, left leg bouncing nervously as I stare at the back of Deke's head. It would've been smart of them to put me in the front seat where Agent Kelly could keep me honest, but as it stands, if things go bad, I'm within an arm's distance of snapping the old man's neck if I need to.

I figure that'll take less than a half-second, which will leave me with plenty of time to take care of her, too. We'll see.

Things are quiet at the moment. Deke navigates

the traffic with ease, which tells me he's used to the hustle-bustle of city driving. Whether it's from living around *here* or not is another story altogether. I'd say most of their kind are residents of the northern Virginia area where a lot of the big government offices are, but it's possible that they're stationed out west.

That idea changes when he has to ask me for road clarifications a couple of times once we cross the river and head into Vancouver, Washington. It could be an act, but I doubt it, because Agent Kelly doesn't offer up any solid knowledge either.

Why does this matter? It doesn't, really, but I like to know that my handlers are confident of their surroundings. If they're operating with some level of ignorance, what else don't they know? I like to see the bottom of the pool before I dive in, you know? That's the one good thing about the CIA, NSA, and the FBI—this might sound unbelievable, but when it comes to doing what I do for them…total transparency.

That took years to earn.

With Agent Kelly, Deke, and the DPS, however, I'm back to rookie status, and I'm not feeling the love.

***

Once we're a ways north of Vancouver and traveling along the Columbia River, Deke pulls into a rest area. "Anybody need to rest?" he asks and actually chuckles at his own joke.

Agent Kelly and I both say no, and Deke offers more detail than he needs to about being old, bladder size, and nature calling. When he gets out of the car, he leans back inside and says to her, "We're probably close enough. Give him the thing." Deke slams the door closed and does the full-bladder waddle across the parking lot.

"The thing?" I ask.

"Trust me," Agent Kelly says, "it's for your own good," as she hands me a black cloth bag with a gold drawstring. I've seen these before, and they're usually worn by SALCON detainees in some exotic prison halfway around the world. I've heard Thailand is nice if you're an illegally detained prisoner.

I toss it back to her. "I'm not wearing that." Out the window, a young mother and father chase their darting, giggling children between a minivan and a pickup. They're laughing and having a good time. He's probably a computer programmer. She works as…I'm going to guess as a caterer—a little dessert company that specializes in cupcakes. Their kids are both towheaded, about five or six years old, a boy and a girl.

SUPER

American dream, right? I'm jealous. Maybe I'll have that one of these days.

But first, these people want me to kill Patriotman and catch an international traitor.

My appointment calendar should be booked solid for April.

Agent Kelly hands the black hood over the seat and says, "To get what you want, you will, Leo. You asked to talk to the suits; that's what we're giving you. I made the calls. I didn't have to."

Her demeanor has changed. She's all business; gone is the friendly *who's-your-buddy* woman that I had already married in my mind. I snatch it from her hand with enough force to show her I'm irritated. "Fine."

But no Belize for you.

I hold up the black hood and examine it. "I've always wondered…who makes these things? I mean, like, do you buy them in bulk from Abercrombie & Terrorist or what? Or maybe they're hand sewn by the indigenous people of wherever and smuggled in on the back of a donkey?"

She wiggles around in the passenger seat so that she's facing me. With an upturned eyebrow, she asks, "What're you talking about?"

"Have you never wondered just how much stuff goes into making the world go 'round?"

"No. I prefer to stay blissfully ignorant."

"But you work for an intelligence agency."

"Like I said…blissfully ignorant."

"Seriously, think about it," I say, sitting forward in the back seat, close enough that I could grab her hand, break her thumb, and have her subdued before Deke pulls his zipper up.

I won't, though. Not yet.

I hold up the hood. "There's a guy that makes the string that goes into the mouth of this hood. Somebody feeds cloth into a machine and it spits this thing out. Then, somewhere back at the zero point, there's a guy in a factory whose sole job is to monitor the assembly line where a bolt is made that holds the wings on an airplane. Some guy has to put the bolt on the plane along with the other millions of parts, and then another guy loads boxes of black hoods into the cargo bay, and—"

"And five hundred million years ago a dinosaur died to make the oil that goes into the engine, and now it's there in your hand. I get it. What's your point?"

I'm not sure I have one. The number of things that had to happen to get that black sack into my hands is mind numbing, but I make something up to sound smart.

I pull it on and let it rest on my forehead. "We're

all living in one big machine, Agent Kelly. Whether it happens by design or by accident, things happened in order to get us right here, right where we're sitting. We're living in a machine that continues to function even if some of the parts are broken. Humanity tries to steer it in the directions we want to go, but does it matter what we do? There's really only one direction we *can* go, and that's forward, no matter what happens."

"I still don't see your point."

"If that guy making the bolts died, it wouldn't change a damn thing about the direction we're all headed. We're going forward regardless, at least until some outside force changes it for us, so if that's the case then why does it matter if I see how we get to where we're going? And furthermore, why does Patriotman have to die if the world won't stop?"

I'll have to admit, I'm having a hard time with what they're asking me to do.

"That's exactly the point, Leo. If the end result is the same, then why not make a few changes along the way to make it better? And you can spew out whatever philosophy you want. The reason for the hood is simple: cause and effect. *You* wear the fucking thing, so *I* don't lose my job. You *don't* wear it, I put a bullet between your eyes, and we find someone else to complete the mission. The world keeps turning, just like you said."

That doesn't exactly explain why I have to eliminate the most beloved superhero in the history of mankind, but whatever. I like my job, and I like my forehead free of gaping holes. Round Two goes to Agent Kelly, so I sit back, pull the black hood all the way down over my head, and cinch the string tight.

"Lie down on the seat," she tells me. "If I have to murder that family because they saw you, that'll be a very bad day, and I don't appreciate very bad days."

I understand what she's getting at, but man, those are some harsh threats coming from a representative of the federal government whose job is to protect people.

The car door opens, and Deke grunts his approval. "Much trouble?"

"He fits his profile so well, it's like he's acting out scenes from a script. They'll be pleased."

My voice is muffled coming through the black cloth, but I say it loud enough for them to hear, "I'm not deaf, you know."

But, I'm also concerned about who "they" are and why "they" will be pleased at the apparent lack of deviation from my norm.

***

We travel maybe another fifteen minutes. I feel the car decelerate down an exit ramp, we make a right turn, heading east, and then who knows where we end up, because Deke makes so many rights and lefts and stops and U-turns that I have to assume he's doing it on purpose. He must figure that if I'm a good judge of distance, based on where we stopped at the rest area, I could find my way back here.

He's right. I could've, if it hadn't been for the haphazard insanity he just pulled. Well played, Deke. Another round for the defending champs.

Five more minutes pass before he parks the car. They climb out, and that's followed by the right side door opening near my head. Agent Kelly says, "Out, Leo. We're here. Leave the hood in the car."

I do as she says, and when I exit and get to my feet, it's not what I expect, but it kind of is at the same time. It's wet and flush with green everywhere; a thick grove of pine trees envelops the surrounding area. It smells like wet earth and drenched pine needles. Behind me, a road cuts through the evergreen forest, and, faintly, the hum of traffic on a highway cuts through the thick fog. I couldn't even begin to guess where we are.

We're in the middle-of-nowhere Washington. I wish there were some sort of landmark nearby to give me a hint, or the scent of salt air to know we're closer to the ocean, but with such a short drive time, we're still deep in the pine jungle.

I could get home if you gave me a compass, but since that's not an option, I'm here, and I might as well be moving forward.

When I turn, the large home in front of me is surprising. I had anticipated a dull, boxy, beige-colored government building with minimal windows and plentiful soul-sucking attributes like a spot reserved for the DPS director of Northwest Operations or some nonsense.

Nope. This place is gorgeous; mossy, gray siding covers the outside, accentuated by black shutters and white trim. Potted plants hang from baskets, flowers bloom beautifully, while the small bushes lining the walkway are carved into miniature shapes. I see a puppy, an angel, and what appears to be a sailboat before Agent Kelly grabs me by the upper arm and drags me toward the house.

Deke follows, but since it's on a slight incline, I can hear him already struggling to keep up behind us.

I pull my arm free of her talon-like grip and say, "I'm guessing this isn't an officially sanctioned building, huh?"

"Black site," she says, keeping her eyes trained on

the looming porch steps. "You didn't think we'd just parade you through the front door of our corporate headquarters, did you?"

"I didn't expect a marching band, but I wasn't prepared for my grandparents' house, either."

"Time to behave, then, because we're about to meet Grandma and Grandpa."

Being younger and fitter, we take the steps in twos while Deke latches onto the handrail and propels himself upward with willpower and grunts.

Agent Kelly knocks on the door's window, and it rattles loosely. I fall into old habits, doing a quick visual recon of the area.

Pine trees and…and that's about it. I see no other cars aside from the black sedan, which sits in the driveway, engine ticking as it cools down.

If we're meeting someone, how'd *they* get here?

When the front door finally opens, I don't have to wonder how. I *know* how.

Deke and Agent Kelly appear to be as surprised as I am.

SEVEN

Present Day

I've lost track, but I think I'm about four scotches in, and I've explained every single detail I can think of to Phil. He's playing some Lou Reed on the stereo and at times, I haven't been able to figure out if he's listening to me or *Walk on the Wild Side*.

He's matched me drink for drink, yet his cheeks aren't rosy, and you'd never be able to tell he'd had a sip if it weren't for the half empty bottle he's cradling like a football. He stopped making eye contact with me ten minutes ago, which I presume to mean that he's so disgusted with my actions that he can't even look in my direction.

I say, "And that's it. Charlene's got a hard-on for Liar Liar Pants on Fire Dallas, both of them apparently work for DPS, and, somehow, Charlene knows the details of my mission, or *missions*, plural, but I don't know what to believe anymore."

The words come out more slurred than I like. Liquor doesn't mix well with me, and as it stands, I'm calling a cab when I leave here. Or, I could steal the Hummer parked outside. Around here, who would care if I ditched it in the Willamette River?

Phil stays silent for so long, the bobbing diver in his fish tank goes through four iterations of surfacing and sinking. The gentle gurgling is almost relaxing. I have to admit though that watching that little dude under the water makes me feel like I'm drowning. My chest is heavy, and I can't take a full breath. This isn't like me. The house-of-cards espionage happening all around me stands on shaky ground. I don't get myself into these situations. I'm smarter than this.

Phil runs a finger across his lips. He sighs and checks the bottom of his empty glass, then sets it to the side.

Thank God, because I'm ready to call mercy.

Once he finally looks at me, he says, "When you started this, I told you—no, I *begged* you to stay smart, and you swore to me that you would. You swore. I promised your mother that you'd be fine. Anybody with a head as hard as yours has to be stubborn enough to stay alive just to piss off everyone else. I told her, 'When the big bombs drop, the only things left will be Leo and the cockroaches.' She bought it, every word of it. But now, goddamn it, Leo, if you don't live to see the end of the week, score one for the cockroaches."

Phil is that grumpy old man who's seen everything

and knows that the world can be a shitty place, but he's normally not so gloom and doom. Anybody that can ask my mother to come back after twenty years of affairs has to be a guy who's filled with so much lofty hope, his damn feet don't touch the ground.

He's always encouraged me, particularly when I was an idiot teenager trying to find my path, so this lack of *go-get-em-sonny-boy* is disconcerting.

I say, "It's that bad, you think?" I try to stand up and the world spins on an alcohol-propelled axis. I allow gravity to pull me back down. It's safer in the chair.

"I've always told you the truth, haven't I?"

"Mostly."

"And if I lied, it was for your own good. Like that time you were in high school; I told you Ellie Tolliver was kissing that boy out behind the Tastee-Freeze. She would've ruined you."

That's a long story that we don't need to get into.

"I don't like the sound of it, Leo. I don't, not at all. And let me see if I heard you right. Two strange people approached you in the airport, they didn't wave any credentials, and you took their word that they were from some top-secret group that's *so* top secret, even the president hasn't heard of them? I got some

oceanfront property in Colorado if you're that
gullible."

"I thought that—"

"No, you didn't. You didn't *think* at all. First, they
tell you there's a traitor in your little group of nimbly-
pimbly boo-hoos, and they want you to find out who it
is, and then oh, by the way, since you work for us now
we need you to take out the only superhero left with
more common decency than what's in his pinky finger.
That didn't sound fishy to you?"

"Of course it did." I'm woozy from the scotch. My
cheeks are flushed warm, and I sink back into the
comfy couch. All I want to do is close my eyes. It's
been a hell of a month, and I'm no closer to finding
out who the real traitor might be. Something sparks
way down deep in my mind like striking flint together.
It's not much, and I can't feel it growing any clearer.

"Then why'd you take the job?"

"The money." I'm drifting, barely able to stay in
the land of the sober, but I'm still aware enough to tell
him my own lies. "It's always about the money."

It's never about the money, but Phil is right. I'm
one stubborn son of a gun, and I've never disobeyed
my gut instincts. That's how I've survived this long,
but, when Agent Kelly and Deke Carter showed me a
check with an extra comma in it, I didn't hesitate when

I should've. I disobeyed my own principles.

Yet, when it comes to enough money to fund your retirement for good, the word "sanity" isn't spelled with a dollar sign.

I'm ready to teeter off the edge into drunken slumber when I hear Phil say something about my mother, forgiveness, second chances, and that he'll make some calls.

I dream about Dallas in that white pantsuit. She's somewhere in the Maldives, having lunch with Charlene. They're sitting in a bar out over the pristine blue water, laughing and sipping fruity drinks while I observe them from a nearby table.

Deke and Agent Kelly show up. Handshakes and hugs are exchanged as an unidentified male approaches. It's only when he turns that I realize he's the man who opened the door at the DPS black site. Someone says my name and laughter erupts from the table.

I wake up, thinking I'm in a cold sweat. I blink my eyes and grasp that Phil has poured a glass of water on me. I groan, asking him if that was really necessary. "You could've just said my name, you know."

"What fun would that be?"

"You said something about making calls last night. Anything?"

Phil doesn't answer. Instead, he turns toward the kitchen and tells me to follow him. I stumble down the hallway, my teeth feeling like they're wearing sweaters, and I'm dying to get rid of this sour taste on my tongue. I smell coffee and the mere scent of it perks me up. Phil tells me to sit, then pours me a mug of the dark stuff and hands me a cup of water and two white pills to go along with it.

The steam pours up and I sip gingerly, trying not to burn my tongue.

Phil looks at me with a measure of relief and annoyance. How he gets his face into that position is anybody's guess. I figure you have to be a parent to pull it off. He says, "First, you're fortunate."

I set the mug down. "Why?"

"Six of my contacts have heard of the DPS, which is a good thing. It means they're legit and you got lucky enough to take a job from a real organization."

"Meaning?"

"Could've been some terrorist group or maybe even some SALCON reps trying to flush out the guy who put a shank in Patriotman."

"It wasn't a shank." I hadn't thought of that possibility. I'm learning that I'm way too trusting of my government agencies. Or am I simply slipping? I've been at this for three years. It puts a lot of stress on your mind, always sneaking around, hiding your identity, trying to remember which fake passport you're currently carrying. Will I be Jim Blount today, or am I Mark Tanner? Am I waking up in Chicago or Phnom Penh?

Phil continues, "They tell me that the DPS is new, only been around about eight months or so. Dark agency that handles the threats that nobody wants to touch because otherwise, it'd be a public relations nightmare. That's why they're so underground. DPS doesn't mind getting their hands dirty, and, according to my people, they figure the less anybody knows, the better, *including* the President."

"Any jobs I'd know about?"

"None that *look* like jobs. That girl that was kidnapped in D.C. back in January? Remember her? Pretty blonde that was all over the news?"

"Yeah, Amy…something."

"My guys don't know for certain, but they say that's got DPS written all over it. That intern had intimate knowledge of how far the Vice President stretched out on a ruler, if you get my drift."

"So the agents with DPS are like the mop-up guys?"

"More or less. They handle the dirty work but take on some big time threats, too: stuff that would send the country into a shit-flinging panic if word got out. Say a suitcase nuke goes missing from a warehouse in Tulsa. Calls are made from the higher ups for DPS to take care of it, because with the FBI, CIA—too many damn channels to keep quiet. It's all over the media before sunset."

I take another sip of coffee. I sort of expected this, given the man I met at the black site, but it doesn't change anything. I was stupid enough to blindly follow their orders when I should've come to Phil first.

"So," Phil says, "for right now, we don't have to worry about you getting tortured in some SALCON prison. I gotta admit, though, when you were telling me about Kelly and Carter putting that hood on your head to go see you-know-who, it made me wonder."

After I revealed the identity last night, saying the name out loud, Phil nearly popped a blood vessel and insisted that we never speak it again. Parabolic mics, microscopic bugs, or any high-tech listening device like that could cause bullets to fly if they knew whom we were talking about.

"Here's what's bothering me, son—what?"

"You called me 'son.'"

"Don't get used to it." Phil gets up from the table, groans and rubs his back, and grabs two plain English muffins sitting on the counter. He knows I like them straight out of the bag. We've both eaten them the same way since day one. He hands mine over and says around a mouthful of his own, "They come to you and say, 'We've got a traitor in close quarters, somebody that plans to blow up the White House,' and that's all well and good. Back when I was in and working the home turf we probably followed leads like that fifteen, twenty times a day. Jokers all around the world try to dip their hand in that honey pot because it's an easy target and easy to get us hopping on planes to follow up. Mostly they were empty threats just to cause a little disharmony.

"Now, I can't figure it out," he continues, "because it seems to me that if they had it narrowed down to the eleven other boo-hoos in your sassy group, why not just put an agent on each one? Normally the suits are chasing thousands of these leads each year, right? Why would they need to recruit you if they had less than a dozen options? It seems like a lot of extra effort and paperwork to bring you in the plot, don't you think?"

He's making a lot of sense, and it's something I hadn't really thought through. Not once in the past thirty days has this thought crossed my mind. Truth be told, that's why I hire Phil—he does this kind of thinking for me. I'm good at disappearing in dark alleys, slinking into apartments undetected, and getting close enough to Patriotman to squeeze liquidized brozantium into his ear canal, but, the more Phil talks, the more I realize that I'm damn lucky to be alive.

I lean back in the chair, gnawing on a mouthful of English muffin, and stare out the back window. It's another beautiful day in Portland; hazy, socked-in fog with a light mist peppering the windows. The muted light still hurts my head, however, and I look away to reduce the pounding in my skull.

I can't remember what I told him last night, so I might be repeating myself. I tell him, "They specifically said that they knew it was one of the eleven, they didn't know who, and they couldn't get close enough because if somebody made them, it'd set off too many red flags. You gotta remember, Dad—Phil—those people in my…that group…they might be a little messed up in the head, but they're highly trained assassins that work with people at the uppermost levels of national security. A superhero gets out of whack, any one of those guys might get a direct-line call from the head of the NSA. The DPS knows they're all valuable resources, so if any of the big-time suits got wind that they were snooping around, trying to eliminate an asset—even if that asset had credibly threatened the President—the pissing match would clog up the system for months. It's no secret that Palmer's approval rating is in the single digits, so it wouldn't surprise me if the Holy Triumvirate would allow it to happen on sheer principle. Hell, they might even encourage—holy shit."

Phil looks at me expectantly.

I'm out of the kitchen and down the hallway before I think to yell over my shoulder, "See if you can find any connection between George Silver and the assassins in the support group."

He yells back at me, something about not repeating that name out loud, but I can't make it out because the screen door slams, and I'm thundering down the front steps in twos.

EIGHT

Three Weeks Earlier, Con't.

I'm sitting across from the Secretary of Defense, George Silver, and over his right shoulder and out the window, I can see the official government helicopter sitting on a concrete landing pad. He's wearing a dark green flight suit and a smile, so I can only assume that he flew it here himself for the meeting.

Best guess is, he was at the ceremonial opening of a new defense contractor's building in Seattle. I remember seeing something about it on *Tonight with Don Donner* last week. He has one agent with him on detail, and the guy stands in the corner like an uptight statue, unnecessarily wearing his dark shades in the dim light of somebody's former home.

The place has been gutted, and the only things that remain are the table and chairs where we now sit. I can see faded spots on the walls where pictures used to hang, but that's about it for remnants of a once-lived life. Flames were already dancing off logs in the fireplace when we entered. For that, I'm thankful, because I can almost see my breath. It's chilly up here in the mountains.

George Silver listens politely while Agent Kelly apologizes—blathers, really—for dragging him away from his mini-vacation in Seattle. She asks him how the ceremonial opening went and insists that she expected the director of DPS, Dan Clavell, who was conveniently in the Northwest for another mission debriefing, to be here instead.

"Oh, don't worry about it, Agent Kelly." He gives her the *pffft* hand-wave, and I'm pretty sure I see a twinkle in his eyes. I've seen the guy on television before, talking to reporters about the state of North Korea and Russia, or whichever evil dictator is currently *en vogue* at the moment, and I have to say, he's a handsome devil on television, but in person, he's mesmerizing. Bright blue eyes, full head of sparkling white politician hair, and a million-watt grin all add credence to the fact that this dude is one smooth snake charmer.

"But, sir," she professes, "this is… I don't know, higher up the chain than I expected."

"Who do you think squirrels away the funding for your paycheck, Agent Kelly? Director Clavell is just there to move the white and black pieces around the board." He turns to me, smiles, and I can't help it, I'm taken in by his charisma as well. He says to me, "Deke and Lisa were kind enough to pass along your concerns, Mr. Craft. What can I do for you? Or should I call you Leo? Is that okay?"

He maintains eye contact, warm and friendly, and he moves in closer like he's completely and entirely interested in what I have to say, as if I'm the only person in the room. I know this tactic—I've used it a few times myself—and it's something that Bill Clinton and Steve Jobs are, and were, famous for: the reality distortion field. It's nothing more than some trick of manufactured allure, and I'm aware of this, but damn it's hard to ignore it when a master is laying it on thick.

I clear my throat and sit up. I can't believe I'm about to do this. One way to overcome his tactics is to fire right back at him. Leaning in closer, up on my elbows and smiling, I maintain eye contact and say, "Leo is fine, sir. And is it cool if I call you George? We're all buddies here, right? Same team?"

His face is frozen in that perpetual smile, but the flicker of his eyelids gives him away. He's not used to being treated like this. Shock and awe with magnetism, that's *his* game. Regardless, he says, "My friends call me Sparky. Are we *friends*, Leo?"

"Absolutely. Does that nickname come from the superhero that died in the fifties? That electricity guy that could shoot lightning from his fingertips?"

"Air Force call sign," he says. I think I might

actually win this battle of wills, because he leans back into his creaky chair and tents his fingertips. He rests his chin on his thumbs and asks, "What can we do to help each other?"

Believe me, I notice that he switches from "What can I do for you?" to "How can we help each other?" and it further solidifies how slick he is.

I answer, "As you know, Sparky, our friends here," indicating Deke and Agent Kelly, "they've procured my services for a couple of big, big missions."

"Yes, yes, I'm aware."

It occurs to me that I haven't really planned ahead well enough. I had an idea of what I was going to say, but I'm reminded of that late 1800s Prussian army guy who said something like, "*No battle plan survives first contact with the enemy.*"

I stutter and stumble through the start of about four different sentences before I hold up a hand, close my eyes, and say, "Forget finding out who wants to kill the President for a minute. That's, like, a Tuesday afternoon in my pajamas." Which is kind of a lie because I'm no closer to unearthing any clues than I was a week ago. I open my eyes and lean as far across the table as I can without climbing on it. "But, for the love of God, you people want me to kill Patriotman? *Patriotman?* Why?"

"I was informed that Deke and Lisa explained our reasoning."

I shake my head, sit back, and cross my arms. "Nope. Not good enough. You don't take out Patriotman for threatening to boycott some NATO and SALCON circle jerk. It's not that big of a deal."

Silver lifts a shoulder in a semi-shrug. "And would it make any difference if I told you that Patriotman has been a vocal opposition to the new cross-program policies that the entire world is trying to implement? It's been extremely detrimental to the president's plans."

It's true, Patriotman has been exceedingly vocal about that, and I wholeheartedly agree with his stance.

I study Silver, trying to pick up on any of his microexpressions to see if he's feeding me a line of bull. I spot nothing. Either he's good, or he believes what he's saying. I risk digging further anyway by saying, "You and I both know that those policies will never work. Patriotman's right—he's not even a member of SALCON and he's right. If it's not separation of church and state, it's separation of state and super-state. Ne'er the twain shall meet."

From the corner of my eye, I spot Deke grinning. There's a chance he'll come around yet. Agent Kelly

clears her throat, admonishing me, and Silver holds his
palm up.

"Agent Kelly?"

"Sir?"

"You and Deke can give us a minute. Take Benson
with you." At the sound of his name, the guardian
agent tilts his head in our direction.

Agent Kelly says, "Sir, I'm not so sure that's a
good—"

"The man asked for the truth. He's getting the
truth. We're on a timeline here, and if it means making
certain concessions, then so be it."

"But, sir—"

"Out, Lisa. Deke, you too. Get Benson to tell you
about that time he burned down that village in
Pakistan. Helluva story."

Agent Kelly opens her mouth to protest again,
wisely thinks better of it, and gets up from the table.
Deke gives me a look that has too many undercurrents
to decipher and follows her toward the front entrance.
Benson trails them and pulls the door closed behind
him as he goes.

Silver looks out the window and takes a deep
breath. With everyone gone, he seems weary once he
exhales. His shoulders go limp and he rubs his eyes.
"I'm tired, Leo."

I want to say *So what, who isn't?* but I let it go. Instead, I tell him, "I'm sure there's a lot of pressure in your line of work, huh?" It's an innocuous, throwaway statement, but what in the hell do you say to the guy who jousts other world leaders with his junk in one hand and a machine gun in the other?

"You can't even imagine, son. Every day, we're on the brink of war, and nobody ever sees it. We feed the media piles of bullshit about how everything is hunky dory, and we're shaking hands and kissing babies with the Prime Minister of Whogivesafuckistan, when in reality, that robe-wearing dickwad is threatening to blow up half of Israel if we don't clear some trade sanctions and send his people a few extra bags of rice. It's insane what goes on. So much ridiculous nonsense that the public never sees. Every day—every goddamn day—I'm out there cutting deals to keep the bombs in their silos because, let me tell you, brother, we are one red button away from total annihilation."

"Then you'll forgive me for nudging you along, Sparky, but you said we're on a timeline. What does any of that have to do with me, Patriotman, or one of the jokers in that support group who's supposedly ready to send a missile from Whogivesafuckistan into the White House? That's why I'm here; that's what I want to know."

George Silver, United States Secretary of Defense, and one of the most powerful men in the world, bites his bottom lip, puts his face in his hands, and begins to sob.

***

The car ride home is filled with questions from Agent Kelly. Deke drives quietly while she leans over the seat and fires one after another. What did he say? I can't believe he told you and not us; why would he do that? Doesn't he understand that this is a matter of national security? Aren't you going to say something? You do realize you work for us and that we sign the paycheck?

I ignore all of them. I tell her only that Silver asked me to keep this national secret just that, a secret, because the implications are so overwhelming that dozens of hands around the world will reach for that big red button if anyone finds out.

That really sends her into another tizzy, and she berates me about chain of command and how information should be shared between subordinates and superiors and eventually, she gets to a point where she's not even yelling at me. She's yelling at the sheer injustice of it, period, and it doesn't have a thing to do with my situation. She's pissed at the director of DPS, she's pissed at George Silver for putting her in a potentially harmful situation without the proper details, and she's seriously pissed at Deke for agreeing that if I was ordered to keep my mouth shut, that's exactly what I should do.

"And," Deke adds, "it was your idea to *let* him speak to the suits anyway."

This turns her cheeks flame red. Agent Kelly goes on another tirade, and something she says catches my attention. "Patriotman was never supposed to be a part of this."

"What does that mean?" I ask.

She turns her attention back to the front window and spits out, "Nothing."

"No, that's something. What're you talking about?"

"You don't feel like sharing what Silver said, well neither do I, so let's just leave it at that."

Agent Kelly has a point, and I'm not willing to share what I know in order to hear her secrets. Or am I?

What would be the significance of it? What did she mean that Patriotman was never supposed to be a part of this...this *what?*

Tirade over, the car has gone silent. I stare out the

window as we drive, watching the trees and cars pass in a blur, taking a trip through my memory and trying to recall every detail she gave me.

Okay, so, we were at that country-western joint… The Blazers were on. Deke was up at the bar, drinking a beer. She was sitting across from me and said, what was it… 'We have reason to believe that one of your friends is a traitor.'

And then I said something about not having any friends…

'Acquaintances, then. Somebody you likely know.'

I told her I don't make a habit of rubbing elbows with the bad guys. I mean, hell, I guess you could say that I am the villain, in a way.

What was it she said next? She had a drink of her beer, and then…

'You call yourselves S.A.'s, right? Superhero assassins?

'Yeah. But that's always kind of misleading because we're not assassins that are superheroes. It's just easier to say.'

'Right. And you're familiar with most everyone working in this field?'

'To a point. I know codenames, real names, faces. That's it. It's not like we get together for wine tasting once a month.'

'Did you know that a group of your colleagues have a support group?'

I remember being shocked by that. We're all such hard-asses. Then I remember saying… 'News to me. What's it for?'

'Anxiety. Depression. Their psych profiles suggest they're

having a difficult time performing. Over time, eliminating a perceived hero, no matter how much their deaths are justified, really puts a strain on them. Enough that there's been underground chatter about taking out the President and ending this crusade. Problem is, we have no idea who.'

'No shit?'

'And that's why you're here, Leo. All signs indicate you're a heartless bastard who'll kill anything as long as there are some extra zeroes on the paycheck. Betray one of your own, and we'll make it worth your while.'

That's how it went down, and as I sit here in the back of this sedan that smells like Deke's aftershave, what really bothers me about the situation is not killing one of my own—a lot of them probably deserve to be pushing up daisies—it's the fact that she called me a heartless bastard.

Come on. That's a bit harsh. I'm just digging the ditches that need to be dug.

NINE

Present Day

Point blank, George Silver lied to me that day in the cabin, and I knew that he did, but, damn, he was trying hard to be convincing with all those tears. That bit about how Patriotman had killed the American dream of life, liberty, and the pursuit of happiness by switching sides, by hating President Palmer and SALCON so much that he joined forces with the North Koreans and "became a commie bastard" sounded so persuasive, so real, that he almost had *me* convinced.

It's not often you get the Secretary of Defense bawling about how America is going to shit—and that it's already gone to shit enough for the All-American Hero to shake hands with the devil.

The rest of his story went like this: someone under the President's command had already tried to recruit one of the assassins to take out Patriotman before he could go public with his decision to abandon the American way of life.

He told me that Patriotman uncovered the plan and had done such an excellent job of convincing his would-be murderer that his decisions were for the greater good, he'd turned *that* person against the United States.

Within a month, Patriotman was going to renounce his citizenship, publicly pledge faith to the red flag of doom, and this mystery person in my group would turn the White House, and President Palmer, into a fine mist and leave only a hole in the ground.

Of course, I questioned it as I sat there with him. Of course, it was fantastically unbelievable that the man who is universally beloved, who has come to embody every sense of nationalistic pride, would turn his back on the people he'd sworn to defend.

Silver told me they had no idea who the member of SASS was that had been recruited, only that they had narrowed it down to one of the twelve.

As I rush away from Phil's house, it occurs to me that I might have a pretty good idea of who Silver might be trying to blame, and that Phil likely isn't going to find a connection to any other member of SASS.

***

I land at Dulles International in northern Virginia.

It's late, and I'm tired, but I don't care if it's two o'clock in the morning or not, I'm going after them one by one.

Who? Eric Landers, Joe Gaylord, and Conner Carson, the heads of the NSA, the CIA, and the FBI; one of them has to know something. They didn't just hand me over to the DPS without reason. They would never do it on their own. At least, I don't think they would. We're more than colleagues. We're friends.

Friends by proxy, I suppose, because they've asked me to do lots of inglorious shit to some of the world's most adored superheroes, and I've kept their secrets because that's what I get paid to do, but damn, they wouldn't do what I suspect them of contributing to…would they?

I climb into the rental car and flop down on the soft leather seats. It's got that new-car smell, but the last person that was in here left behind a hint of perfume that reminds me of Shelby. She was the first woman I dared to reveal my job requirements to, and once wasn't enough to learn my lesson.

Man, I'm exhausted. I had spent most of the day back in Portland, driving in circles, thinking and coming up with no decent leads or solutions. Phil called twice and got nowhere either. I let him in on my theory, and he agreed that it was certainly plausible, which is why I'm here in northern Virginia instead of at home, sleeping in my own bed.

I've been paranoid all day that I'm under surveillance, and there's even a little part of me that's scared to turn the key in the ignition.

You know what? Better safe than sorry.

I realize I must look like a fool, but now that I'm down here underneath the car, checking for flashing red blips or any wires that might lead to a bomb, I feel better. That minor surge of adrenaline gives me another boost. It's just after eleven back home, and my body hasn't adjusted yet.

And, given the circumstances, if I'm awake, Eric, Joe, and Conner might as well be too, right?

I leave the airport parking lot, heading for a super rich area of Alexandria where I know Eric Landers, head of the NSA, lives in a three-story home so large that it could house the entire population of New Guinea.

D.C. is dead this time of night, and I love it when it's like this. I spent about two years here, and if it hadn't been for the pure insanity of the go-go-go world everyone here inhabits, I might've stuck around.

It's foggy, too, adding a certain gloomy touch to the quiet city and surrounding suburbs. Stoplights cast green, yellow, and red halos as they cycle through their routines, and it strikes me how odd it is that we're conditioned to obey these things, even in the dead of night, when barely anyone is awake. This is D.C., though, and there's enough traffic on the roads to keep up the tradition of traffic laws.

I drive with the radio tuned to some talk show as a distraction. It works until I see a billboard along the highway. The model—I think it's for shampoo—is a ravishing redhead with a smile that doesn't need giant bulbs to light up her face. It makes me think of Charlene. I'm wary of her, considering she's supposedly with DPS and knows more about me than she should, yet I feel that tug of longing.

Different world, different time, different jobs— you mix all those together magically, and we might have a chance. I don't know this, obviously, because we've never spoken much outside of Group Sharing. It's a feeling. A strong notion of connection, and I'm sure she feels it, too. That's why she was concerned about Dallas stealing my glory. She was feeling protective of me.

Charlene. There are too many questions about her that don't have answers.

I need to think about something else.

The radio doesn't help much. Elevator music signals the end of one program and the beginning of another. There's some nighttime DJ spewing talk radio bullshit about how the world is going to end now that Patriotman is dead. "It's the end of humanity as we know it, my friends," says the DJ, "and you voted this guy in. It's all Palmer's fault. Remember that the next time you cast your ballots in November."

All Palmer's fault. If the guy only knew he should be saying, "It's all Leo Craft's fault."

And then something he said strikes me. It's not so much a smack in the face as it is that flickering of kindling catching fire. *"Remember that the next time you vote."*

It's an election year. Palmer's numbers are abysmal.

Would it be a stretch to think this is related to the election?

I toss the idea around and decide that no, it's all too big to be a part of an election rigging scandal. If you're a spin-doctor for the Republican Party, there are easier ways to completely obliterate what little confidence remains in Palmer's ability to run this country. But, as bad as he is, all the talking heads suggest he'll remain in office because the opposition doesn't have anyone suitable enough to run against him.

They should know that it's a risky maneuver for little to no return.

Hmm. That doesn't mean it's entirely out of the question.

If you're a motivated *Vice* President who might be completely sick of having your good name tarnished because of the incompetency of the Grand Poobah, and you don't want to spend four more years cleaning up his messes, and you think you can do a better job…

A car horn honks behind me, and I snap out of my plotting daze. The light above is green, and I wonder how long it's been that way. I hold my hand up apologetically and press down on the gas pedal. The car behind me swings up to my side and in true D.C. hospitality, the driver flips me the bird and yells something in Russian. He's gone before I have a chance to return the gesture.

So many possibilities to choose from and the more I think about it, the more muddled the details become in my mind.

The GPS announces that I'm five miles from my destination and tells me to turn right. I make a left instead and grab a cup of coffee from a dingy convenience store with a sleepy clerk behind the register and a one-eyed Pomeranian flopped on the counter like he's a placemat.

"Nice dog," I tell the woman.

"That's Sparky," she mumbles. "Don't get near him. He's a real bastard."

Funny. I know another Sparky that's a real bastard.

Back in the car, I sit with the engine running, trying to plan my approach to the three men who might be the connecting points of this complicated puzzle. I'm thinking over my plan to visit the head of the NSA first.

I find a pen and a notepad in the glove compartment and start jotting down some notes. It helps me process things thoroughly when I can see it on paper.

Eric Landers is fifty-three years old. He's about a foot taller than I am, which is to say he bumps his head on the moon when it's hanging low in the sky. He's a family man; Dolores is his wife of thirty years, and they have two boys, Mark and Sam, who are a year apart and attend Harvard. Out of my three government contacts, I like Eric the most. He's a bulldog when he needs to be, but he can also flip the switch and be all chummy with you in the same conversation. I've seen him turn an intern into a blubbering mess of tears and then share nachos with the guy ten minutes later.

He bleeds red, white, and blue, and from what I can tell, he's fiercely loyal to President Palmer, considering they were roommates back at West Point. While I'm simply going on election rigging as a theory, I can't see him purposely taking part in it just to get his buddy out of office. Wouldn't happen.

So do I even need to go see him?

Yes. His lack of motive regarding Palmer doesn't mean he's not involved on some other level.

Okay, Eric Landers it is. He should appreciate a visit from his old pal Leo at two-thirty in the morning. Who wouldn't?

***

I didn't actually expect him to be happy about the rude awakening, but I surely didn't expect the vitriol that I receive as he yanks me inside and slams the door behind me.

"What in the blue blazes fuck are you doing here at my house? Are you insane?" He says this with hushed anger, like he's trying not to wake his wife up, but it doesn't work.

A soft, female voice comes down the stairs. I assume she's poking her head over the railing. "Eric? Everything okay?"

He calls up the stairs, "It's fine, Dolly. Work stuff."

"At this hour? It couldn't wait until tomorrow?"

"Just go back to sleep, hon. This won't take long," he says, then turns to me and adds, "will it, Leo?"

I shrug. "Maybe."

"Okay, then," Dolores says. "There's fresh French Roast in the pantry if you need it."

Cheerfully, he replies, "Thanks, dear," and then practically shoves me into the study at my left. I take quick mental notes of the room as he swiftly but quietly shuts the door. Books line shelves, plants hang from hooks, I can see that the windows could use a touch of cleaning, and his desk is cluttered with stacks of manila folders, letters, books, a laptop, a pencil holder, and a family photo in a silver frame.

Eric says, "Do you have any idea how risky this is, coming here? What're you thinking?"

"I need some answers."

"Leo, I'm not sure that—"

"Why does George Silver want Patriotman dead?" I interrupt. "And why is the DPS planning to use me as a scapegoat for whatever else is coming?"

I nearly have to lift him off the ground by his throat before he'll give me an answer.

TEN

Two Weeks Earlier

Okay, so regardless of how ticked off Agent Kelly is, I still have a job to complete.

She was kind enough to remind me that they wired an inordinately large amount of money to my Swiss bank account, which means I should probably get to work—seriously this time—trying to find out which one of my counterparts is a traitorous bastard.

The thing is, I'm starting to wonder whether there's actually someone out to blow up the White House. If Silver was lying to me about Patriotman's involvement, and I know he was, then it could also mean that the other half of this assignment is total bunk, too.

For now, though, I'm going to proceed as if that part of the mission is true, simply because Agent Kelly had no idea what Silver could've told me, and, she said, "Patriotman was never supposed to be a part of this."

It's a stretch, yeah, but stranger things have happened, and if you think about it, it makes sense in a way. Her superiors want Patriotman dead for reasons unrelated to her and Deke's original mission of preventing a presidential assassination attempt, and she's annoyed that they're butting in on her domain. It's a turf war. Has to be. Superiors versus subordinates and yeah, it sucks, which is exactly why I'm an entrepreneur. I like being my own boss.

Sometimes it's a good thing, though, because going back to what I said to her earlier, we'd never make any progress as a society if life weren't one huge pissing match.

Okay, that's settled. We have a wolf in sheep's clothing to find.

And to ensure that Silver knows I'm on board, I've scheduled my trip to the Maldives for later in the week. They've shown a few blurry photos of him, so it's not confirmed that he's officially there, but all the tabloids say that Patriotman is supposedly vacationing in the Maldives until the end of April, and I figure I'll go after I attend another SASS meeting.

My tasks: kill Patriotman and find a domestic terrorist in order to prevent an assassination. Simple enough.

It's not that I'm a fan of President Palmer—however, the guy did have a great platform when he ran on the promise of bolstering education, which I'm all for—but once he was in office, the D.C. machine railroaded him into just another talking head who couldn't get anything passed by the divided House and Senate. They were too interested in seeing who had the biggest *schlongs* to pass any real reform.

I think after a year the guy just got bitter and was burdened by petty jealousy. There were all these superheroes on *Tonight with Don Donner* getting more accolades than the man who was trying to do his best for an entire nation. Some masked muscle man on the street that saved an old lady from a mugger would be handed the keys to a city while every talking head on television skewered poor Palmer. He couldn't take it.

That's my theory, anyway. It wasn't long after his failed attempts at any real reform that the late night phone calls started with secretive, electronically disguised voices placing orders.

They went something like this:

"We're aware of your activities, Mr. Craft, and we'd like you to come work with us. Carl Banks, and you may know him as Gray Ghoul, has been secretly operating with the Russians to sabotage oil pipelines through Eastern Europe. He'll be hard to track down over there, but he's worth three hundred thousand. Plus, get on our good list with this one and there'll be plenty more."

"Deathmarch, a.k.a. Bill Frederickson, had a hand in helping the IRA procure the appropriate items for explosive

devices back in the '80s. He's been on a low-priority wanted list for thirty years, but with his recent work as a hero, we'd been cutting him some slack. It's time for the chickens to come home to roost. Five hundred thousand if you can get rid of him by Thursday."

"Tom Liverpelt, who goes by the handle Captain Kane, has become one of our top priorities in the past week. It involves child pornography, and we can't say more than that. Highest order, Mr. Craft. He's in San Diego for a conference and if you can get it done by tonight, we'll tack on a bonus. Million five."

Before all this started—officially working for the government, I mean—I was on a mission of my own, trying to take out a superhero named BlazeWire who was on the take from some real bad guys.

I'd been undercover for about six weeks, running jobs for the Bandito Cartel down in Mexico, and honestly, it took me a couple of days to make up my mind when I got the first NSA invite, because I couldn't decide who was more dangerous: a bunch of cutthroat bastards holed up in Juarez or the United States government.

So yeah, that's how I got here, and, anyway, that's all beside the point. The President isn't a bad guy, but he's probably a little misguided. I'm not part of Palmer's Army, by any means. Still doesn't mean he deserves to die, even if I have more fingers than he has points in his approval rating.

I'll do my part to make sure he doesn't go on display in a coffin, and in the meantime, I'll try to figure out what's going on with George Silver. Why was he lying to me about Patriotman?

And speaking of which, this "eliminate Patriotman" thing is really cramping my style, too, because it has far more serious implications than I'd like to admit.

Okay, too much going on up in the old gray matter.

I should get the Palmer thing squared away first, then I'll tackle what to do about Patriotman. How do you eat an elephant? One bite at a time.

***

When you're trying to do investigative work on a group of international assassins who are good enough to sneak up on superheroes with abnormal powers—and murder them—it's not like you can simply sit down in a café and hide behind a newspaper and some dark sunglasses.

I learn this quickly, on Day One of Serious Investigation Commencement, when Charlie Delta spots me from across the way during Portland's Saturday Market downtown. He waves at me and strolls over, holding a t-shirt with a screen-printed owl on the front.

I play it off like I'm there to browse the artisanal cheeses and homemade jams in support of all the fantastic local artists. We have a beer together, talk shop, and he tells me he's late for a flight to Guam.

"Apparently," he says, glancing around, making sure no one is eavesdropping, "Green Devil has been trading arms with some underground outfit along the border of Pakistan. Those damn cave dwellers. Can you believe it? I would've never expected Devil to be in on something like that, but all the data points from Homefront indicate it's as true as the sun rising. And you think you know people, huh?"

Pffft. Tell me about it.

"Anyway, I figure I'll catch him in Guam while he's visiting his mama."

"That's cruel."

Charlie Delta shrugs. "You mess with the bull…"

I nod in acknowledgement, trying to study his microexpressions to see if he's hiding anything. Charlie Delta has a long list of accomplishments when it comes to eliminating people on the wrong side of justice, but he's not a murderer.

That sounds weird when I say it like that. The dude kills people for a living.

What I mean is, he doesn't kill the innocent ones. He's a good guy, but I'm not ready to check him off my list.

You think you know people…

That faint smell of damp city wafts over me as Charlie Delta stands up from the table. He pushes his white plastic chair out of the way. The table wobbles, unstable. He offers to shake my hand, which I accept, and then he asks me, "See you at SASS on Tuesday?"

"Wouldn't miss it."

"Good, good." He pauses, nodding somberly, like he's got something to add. He hasn't let go of my hand yet, and it's slightly awkward. He squeezes and shakes again, finally relaxing his grip. "We're all friends there, Leo. Those guys have done a lot of good for me and my mental state. This work is hard, but I don't have to tell you that. Preaching to the choir. Whatever's bothering you, keep your head up. There are plenty of shoulders to cry on." With that, he's gone.

I watch him go, feeling like that was the most genuine thing I've heard out of a human being in a long time. I don't think Charlie Delta is my guy, but I'm not counting him out yet. I'm not counting anybody out.

***

I hop on a quick flight down to SFO because that's where Tara and Mara make their home when they're not travelling the world, killing people for a living. They live in an old 1950s, Eichler-style home, with lots of windows and an open-air courtyard in the middle. Their place has an incredible view of the San Francisco Bay, and to call me jealous would be an understatement. This city is second on my list, but Jesus, who can afford it, even if you have millions of dollars from eliminating superheroes?

The twins are too smart for me to hang out in a warm car, chugging coffee and eating doughnuts, pretending I'm on a stakeout, so what I do is, I walk right up to their front door, and I knock.

Tara comes to the door—and I know it's her because of the chicken pox scar to the right of her nose—and she's wearing pink, flowery pajamas. Her feet are tucked into blue slippers. She smiles and says, "Leo? I didn't know you were in town." I spot Mara behind her, wearing blue, flowery pajamas and pink slippers, sitting at the kitchen table with a cup of coffee.

"I'm just down for the day, looking at some real estate. Figured I'd stop by."

Tara steps to the side and beckons for me to enter. "Come in, come in. Sorry we're in our jammies. We're still recovering."

"From what?" I ask, stepping into the front entryway.

She rolls her eyes. "You would not *believe* the trouble we had with Commander Cro-Magnon in Sydney. It went downhill in a hurry, and, besides, that's a long-ass flight back."

Mara calls to me from the kitchen. "Hey, Leo!" She waves and asks if she can get me a cup of coffee or a scone. When I decline, she gives me the pish-posh scoff and gets up to serve me something anyway.

We sit at their kitchen table, eating the best homemade scone I think I've ever had along with homemade strawberry jam that would rival some of the masters down at the Saturday Market. I ask them how they have time to do all this from scratch, given our schedules, and they pass it off as, "Oh, it's nothing. You should see the energy our mother has, and she's in her mid-seventies."

You'd think that if I were trying to figure out whether or not these two were planning to assassinate President Palmer, I'd be sneakier and more cautious instead of trying the direct approach. While that makes sense, it also makes sense to catch these people unaware, especially Tara and Mara, when they're relaxing in their own environment.

We're all inherently suspicious of everything, even each other, and I can guarantee you that no matter how much they're smiling and sharing their kickass jam, there are at least five different things hidden around this kitchen that would lead to my imminent death if they think anything is shady about me or the reason I'm here.

Tara and Mara tell different parts of the Commander Cro-Magnon story interchangeably, finishing each other's sentences in true, stereotypical, twins-in-a-chewing-gum-commercial fashion, while I sit patiently and study them. They, too, are highly skilled, professional assassins, some of the best in the world, but I'm not getting that gut-bomb vibe that says they're domestic terrorists. Still, they'll remain on the list for now.

Here's why I think that the surveillance and investigations into my SASS counterparts will be easier than I originally expected: my interlude with Charlie Delta leads me to believe that they're all there for a shoulder to cry on, just like he said, and I have two perfectly good ones.

My task is to figure out which one of the eleven is shedding the least amount of tears. It's not these two, so that's three out of the way. Are the ones that are left capable of murdering the President? Definitely, but which one of them has the mindset to do it?

ELEVEN

Present Day

Eric Landers, head of the NSA and one of, if not *the* most powerful intelligence official in the United States of America, sputters and gags underneath my grip. "Let…me…go," he gurgles. Actually, he hisses, but it's hard to tell if he's angry or if it's a byproduct of my vise-like claws around his Adam's apple. I'm going with a combo of both.

"Not until you tell me why."

"Why,"—*cough, gag*—"why *what*, Leo?"

"You know exactly what I'm talking about. Who's setting me up?" He tries to spit out another non-answer, and I finally give up, and let go. This back and forth nonsense will take all night, and besides, the shower of spit is kinda gross, even if it's coming from His Holiness Landers.

He stumbles away from me, rubbing his throat. He's grown a mustache since I last saw him, and flecks of spittle dangle from the hair above his lips. "You think somebody is trying to frame you? For what?"

"You know damn well what. I'm losing my patience with this—"

"Leo, for God's sake. It's three o'clock in the morning, and I have no fucking clue what you're talking about. I can't help you…" he says, pleading with his eyes, his hands, "I *really* can't help you unless you tell me what's going on."

I take a deep breath and snort it out in a frustrated huff. If I were a bull in a rodeo ring, I'd be pawing the ground, preparing to charge the idiot clown hiding in the barrel. I'm tempted to mow him down and leave a puddle of NSA goon juice in my wake, but given the expression on his face, I'm inclined to believe that he might be as clueless as he claims. After all, he supposedly handed me over to the DPS, and they're pretty freaking crappy about sharing information. "Okay, let's back up a bit. Tell me about the DPS."

Landers retreats, holding his palms up to me, shaking his head. "That's beyond my—"

"Eric!"

His hands drop and he looks forlornly at a bottle of scotch sitting on the wet bar. He's been sober for twelve years and that particular bottle keeps him honest. It's a constant test of willpower; at least that's what he's told me before. I couldn't say whether it's true or not, but he's salivating. He resists however, and, instead, he pulls a can of diet soda from the mini-fridge near his thigh. The top hisses when he pops it.

He offers me one, and I decline, telling him to get on with it.

To speed things up, I explain to him what Phil had learned about Direct Protection Services and Landers says, "Then, believe it or not, you know as much as I do."

"You're the head of the NSA, Eric. How can you *not* know about a department that's operating under your nose? You don't have any operatives inside their ranks? You haven't tried to sneak some info? C'mon, I'm not buying it. You probably know what I had for breakfast this morning. How does anything this big get past you?"

"It gets past you when you don't have access, Leo. DPS is all George Silver. He's got his little band of cronies running around, pulling rank on all my agents, stealing my assets," he says, indicating me. "As far as I know, DPS is there to do exactly what your pop said it does. They're sweepers. They clean up messes—the kind of shit the public would go crazy over. Look at me—*look*—I have nothing to do with them."

I back up to his sofa and plop down. I point at a cushy looking armchair and motion for him to sit, too. He shakes his head, tells me he'd rather stand, and moves over to the giant picture window overlooking a lawn the size of a football field. I say, "Then help me figure this out, because the way I see it, right now the DPS has two piles of dirt they're trying to sweep up. First off, these two agents—"

"Kelly and Carter?" he asks with a raised eyebrow.

"Yeah. I thought you didn't know them?"

"Bulldozed their way into my office a couple weeks ago, demanding I hand you over. Balls the size of grapefruits, but she's a looker. Doesn't seem like the type."

"While that may be true, she's shady, Eric. Wild swings on loyalty and sanity. How much do you know? She mentioned she got clearance from you to use me for a while."

"Something about a plot on Palmer. That's all she'd give me. Silver confirmed it when I checked in, but that's all I got."

"She comes to me and says there's a traitor running with the S.A.'s. Somebody's trying to kill the President, and it's one of the people in this support group. Wants me to join it to see if I can find out who."

"Support group?" He turns to me, confused, eyeing me over the rim of his soda can. In the low light of his study, I can tell that he's thoroughly mystified. It feels strange to have more information about something than the head of the NSA.

I smirk. It's not really funny, but damn it's been a long day, and I think I'm starting to get a little loopy. "It's called SASS. The Superhero Assassin Support Society. Almost every S.A. out there working gets together to bitch and moan about how hard this life is."

"No kidding? Isn't that a bit risky? I mean, what if Billie Bombshell showed up? We'd have to recruit and train an entirely new set of you people."

"Glad to hear your *current* assets are valuable, but yeah, I've said the exact same thing. Look, I could go on and on, but it's all unnecessary detail. DPS mess number one is this supposed plot against Palmer's life, and they think it's someone in SASS."

"Do you?"

I lean back and cross my arms. Shaking my head and shrugging at the same time, I answer, "I'm no closer to figuring anything out than I was a month ago. That first week, I thought it'd be a cakewalk. To be an elite bunch of assassins, they're all—every single one of them—they're all as transparent as plastic wrap, but I've got nothing."

"Interesting."

"How so?"

"If somebody tells you there's an idiot in the room and you can't find him…"

I offer a lifeless chuckle. "Then I'm the idiot. That's part of the reason I'm here."

"You think George Silver is setting you up? You really believe he'd dare to get his hands dirty like that?"

I lift a shoulder, let it fall. "I don't know what I believe any more. And that's why I'm here. Answers."

"What's mess number two?" He drains the last of his soda and tosses it into the trashcan, but not before eyeing the scotch bottle. For a second there, I think he was seriously considering it.

I rub my hands together and push myself up from the couch. I hate admitting what I'm about to say, because from the first moment I was recruited to do this, my last mark had been strictly off-limits. He was too good, too pure. Plus, he'd retired and was no longer considered a relevant entity by anyone in the upper echelons of governmental control...at least not until George Silver lied to me about Patriotman's intentions.

I ask, "You've seen the news lately, haven't you?"

Eric leans back with his arms out wide with that look of a disappointed parent, as if I'd gotten busted on a Wal-Mart parking lot for underage drinking. "No, you didn't?"

"I did. I had to."

"Why?"

I lie and tell him, "You know why, Eric. I say no, and the requests stop coming. It's always about the money, and, besides, he'd been out of the game for years. Hadn't done any meaningful work in—God, I couldn't even tell you how long."

Three years, actually, but he doesn't need to know that I've been keeping up with Patriotman. Goddamn, it was like murdering an old friend.

"He was off limits, Leo. You know that."

"Not according to George Silver." I explained George Silver's story to Landers, the one about how Patriotman had intended to side with the North Koreans and had a little bit of a Stockholm Syndrome effect on his would-be assassin—the original one—and now said assassin was doing Patriotman's dirty work for him, or would be, if and when he decided to eliminate President Palmer.

Landers stands there dumbfounded, mouth hanging wide open, unable to process what I'm saying, and I assume it's due to the fact that Patriotman was the very symbol of nationalistic pride. "How could he do such a thing? I don't believe it."

"I couldn't either, but Silver swore it was true."

"Now I'm glad you got rid of the son of a bitch." He puts a hand on his forehead. "All those years, and for what? He turns his back on us the moment we get some nincompoop in office that doesn't know his head from a hole in the ground? Jesus Christ Almighty."

I push myself up from the chair. It's clear that Eric Landers knows nothing. I'm getting zilch accomplished here and I woke the poor bastard up for nothing. "Sorry I wasted your time, Eric. I thought maybe you'd…"

My words trail off because I really don't know what I was thinking, other than the fact that I'd assumed the head of the *fucking NSA* would have some answers. I'm angry with him for being so clueless. I'm angry with myself for wasting precious time.

He moves to the window, puts his hands behind his head, and stares out over the kingdom that is his backyard. "No, no, you're fine," he reassures me. "I wish I had more for you."

"Is there anything you can do for me? Anybody to talk to? Questions to ask?"

"I can make some calls, ask around, but I'll tell you this, Leo, I gotta be careful. This gets on the wrong side of George Silver, I'm out on my ass, maybe even buried."

I move over beside him, study his face, looking for any signs of malfeasance. When he turns to me, there's nothing. He simply looks old and tired, and a bit lost now that there's a group out there with more power than he has.

"So I'm on my own, huh?"

He nods apologetically. "One thing I'm coming back to, Leo—did you know that Silver was *never* a fan of Patriotman?"

"What? No." News to me, because for as far back as I could remember, from his time in the Senate, up through his reign as governor of Virginia, campaigning for the Presidency himself a couple of times, and then finally onto the cabinet, he'd always been the biggest damn proponent of Patriotman among any political figure out there. Hmm. Now that I think about it, maybe that was why he was crying—or pretending to—the dude had to keep up appearances.

You know, before every word out of his mouth was a big fat honking lie.

"He had to play nice on TV because who the fuck doesn't like Patriotman, right? If he came out against the defender of the human race, he would've been crucified by the media. Dead in the water before his political aspirations ever got off the ground."

"It goes back that far?"

"Something like twenty-three years, if my math is right."

"Damn. I was, what, sixteen?"

Yeah, I was sixteen, and I was fairly familiar with Silver, even back then.

I was a big kid, too. I mean, a *big* kid for my age. My classmates called me Pops because I was already shaving and packing on muscle just by looking at weights.

"So what happened?"

Landers turns to me. Just as he opens his mouth, a red dot blinks onto his forehead.

The insane thing is, I know exactly what this is— I've had them trained on me who knows how many times. I've painted them all over my own targets for the last three years. I know exactly what's about to happen, but I lack the ability to react. My brain is unwilling, or unprepared, for this to happen right in front of me, especially when I'm not the one initiating it.

My arms go numb. My skin prickles. I manage to lift a hand and squeak out a pitiful, "Get d—"

The glass picture window crackles. Landers grunts when a hole opens in his forehead. His body folds in half as he crumples to the floor.

TWELVE

Two Weeks Earlier, Con't.

I tackle my West Coast counterparts for the first couple of days, and so far, I'm batting the biggest zero in the history of batting averages. I've been spinning it as a "new guy wants to get to know you personally" kind of thing, lest they start talking amongst themselves, wondering why the new weirdo is visiting each of them individually.

I've got nothing to show for it.

Which leads me to here—I'm back at home now, in my apartment, preparing to jot down some notes. I've got some white noise playing on my cell to block the sounds of Portland outside; the lights are low, and I can't sleep, which leads me to this: thinking.

It's what I do.

I flip my notebook open and write down eleven names, checking off the S.A.'s I've already visited; then I create a little brainstorm of thought clouds out beside each one.

Charlie Bravo appears to be as clean as the man who shares his name, Charlie Delta. In fact, Charlie

Bravo is even mushier than Charlie Delta about how much SASS has helped him "get through it all," to the point where he's almost crying he's so thankful.

Then, Fred McCracken doesn't come across as fishy in any way, nor do Mike and his wife, Eleanor. They're two of the best assassins in the world, but they wear matching tracksuits for God's sake. She uses curlers and wears a muumuu to bed. Mike, when he's not slipping into some superhero stronghold like an invisible ninja, moonlights as a computer repairman. They're boring in the real world, but they're happy. Why would they want to upset that balance? No matter the size of the paycheck, some people just aren't motivated by the money this job offers.

So, I have to check off both Charlies, the twins Mara and Tara, Fred, Mike, and Eleanor, which leaves Don Weiss, who's even newer than I am, John Conklin, Charlene, and Dallas. Truth be told, my West Coast people are so clean and lacking in motive that for about three hours, I actually weigh the possibility that being so clean is part of the charade.

Like they were *too* innocent. Like maybe they were all in on it, and I'm the odd man out.

That's a dumb idea, though, and I toss it. With so many massive egos—even when they're bruised and looking for comfort—there's no chance in hell that they would all come together to work on something of this magnitude just to trap me.

Would they?

Nah, not a chance.

None, nada, zero. I know these people. I know their type. I can read them all like the back of the shampoo bottle while I'm taking a dump.

What I can't figure out is why any one of them would want to eliminate President Palmer. They simply don't have a reason to unless there are a couple of extra commas in the paycheck, and I can't see them giving up a good living to be on the run for the remainder of their days.

Why go that big? They may have super-sized egos, but they're content to live in the shadows and make bucket-loads of money doing what they do.

Historically, Presidential assassination attempts, both successful and unsuccessful, tend to draw a lot of media attention.

You say the names John Wilkes Booth or Lee Harvey Oswald to anybody over the age of ten, they can tell you who, what, where, and when all these years later.

I can guaran-damn-tee you that none of my cohorts whom I've questioned have any desire to be known on an international level by the time 2164 rolls around.

Say any one of their names five to fifteen decades from now, and they're likely to hope the response would be akin to, "Who the fuck is Fred McCracken?"

Not, "Oh, Fred McCracken! He killed President Palmer in the study with a pipe wrench in 2014."

At this point, I've only been to a handful of SASS meetings, and I can already tell you that I'm not a fan of Dallas, the South Korean woman who suffers from compulsive lying. John Conklin is strange, with a capital "strange" and I'm not sure what his problem is yet. He's fairly new, too, and hasn't opened up much.

Charlene—the attractive redhead—was there for the first meeting I attended, and I haven't seen her since the news broke on *Tonight with Don Donner*. According to the others, she's been dealing with all-encompassing paranoia for a while now, and having her identity revealed on national television can't help. Don Weiss…I don't know much about him.

They're the only four remaining, and they're scattered all over the US. They specifically fly into Portland—as do the Californians—every Tuesday and Thursday evening, just for SASS. I'll have to visit the rest of them later, because right now, I have like three hours to get some sleep before my flight to the other side of the world.

I reach over, flick off my bedside lamp, and then I ponder what I'm about to do.

I'm about to kill off the most beloved superhero in the history of tights, muscles, and masks.

It's bittersweet, if I'm being honest. It's the end of something that meant more to me than just about anyone on this godforsaken planet.

I close my eyes, and the birds begin to chirp outside before a fitful sleep finally comes.

***

When I wake up an hour later, I'm in a state of mild panic because, damn, have I not thought this through. I'm careful, and I'm thorough—really, I swear—but I've had so much on my mind lately that I've failed to properly plan for Patriotman's demise.

See, how this usually works is, like I've said, I get the call with an order from some suit-wearing, smug old bastard like Eric Landers sitting up in Washington. Next, I take a couple of days of prep time, which mostly means I wait on Phil to gather some intel for me while I pack up my gear, drink a few cocktails to calm my nerves, and then wrestle over which fake passport I'm going to use.

Should I get a fake spray tan and dye my hair? Or go with the shaved head and round glasses look of the unassuming Portland hipster? These are the questions I typically grapple with.

Once it's settled, I hop on a plane to France, Thailand, or Lansing, Michigan, where I stalk my prey, catch them in an unfortunate situation like sleeping or showering, and I do the deed. I'm in, I'm out, with no traces left behind, and then the news reports will begin some twelve to forty-eight hours later, depending on how beloved the particular superhero was and how long it took an obsessed fan or relative to find them.

The reporters will generally lead with the blood, and it goes something like this, "On *Tonight with Don Donner*, yet another superhero is brutally murdered in her own home. How long will this savagery continue, and who's behind it? Some say the U.S. government. What do you think? More on the death of the Power Princess after the break. *Tonight's broadcast is sponsored by Sweetums toilet paper…keeps your bottom neat and sweet.*"

If it bleeds, it leads, right? That's how the old saying goes? The truth is, at least in my case—and I can't speak for the others—I tend to lean toward the humane side of the job. A peaceful, resting submergence into the afterlife. There's *rarely* an instance where I have to resort to guns and full-fledged violence.

Seriously, think about it. These people are superheroes for a reason; speed, strength, genetic mutations, billionaires with ultra-cool, one-of-a-kind gadgets, whatever the case, they know a hundred and ninety-two ways to off a bad guy. It's better, trust me, to accomplish your mission undetected. Otherwise, you might find yourself getting tossed around like a sack of potatoes and getting beaten like mashed ones.

I made that mistake once, early on, and I still get pains in my leg on really cold days. Regardless, I'm alive, and yeah, that was an epic battle.

Anyway, the reason I'm panicking is this: Patriotman is supposedly in the Maldives on vacation. It's an extended vacation, really, more like a mini-retirement, and his intent was to come back for another go at fighting crime.

Think of it as Michael Jordan coming back to play for the Wizards, only not as sucky.

While most everyone on the planet will believe whatever manufactured news is on their favorite channel each night, there are others out there—crime units, SALCON, conspiracy theorists—who will question the legitimacy of Patriotman's death.

Why is this a problem?

I need proof. I need a witness.

And I can only think of one credible person that will suffice.

Damn.

***

Kimmie answers the door in a pink tank top and cut-offs made from sweatpants—the ensemble leaves little to the imagination, nipples ripe for nibbling poking through the thin fabric—and as much as I hate to say it, I feel a little wiggle in the worm. If she didn't hate me with the burning rage of a thousand suns, I would find this hard to ignore. Matter of fact, acknowledging her immediate vitriol takes a backseat as I let my gaze linger a half second too long.

She moves to slam the door in my face, but I manage to sneak my arm inside a millisecond before it crushes flesh and bone. It hurts, because she's damn strong for her size, and I almost drop the thick stack of hundreds into her foyer.

Instead, I clinch my fingers tighter around the wad of money and sort of shake it at her as she uses her weight to lean in, smashing my arm. With my nose pressed to the open space between the wall and the door, I say, "I need a favor, Kimmikins."

"Leave, Leo."

"Honey, listen—"

"No. No, no, no, you do *not* get to call me that *ever* again." She grunts and leans into the door, and, I have to admit, I'm seriously considering a full-fledged mission abort.

"Would you stop for a second?" I'm bigger than her—like outweighing her by a hundred pounds bigger—and I could easily use my weight to shove her out of the way, but that would only serve to make her angrier. Plus, if I hurt her, I'll have absolutely zero chance of convincing her to help me out. "Give me thirty seconds."

"No." She grunts, struggles, and shoves.

The good thing is, Kimmie has always been greedy, and motivated by money even though she has plenty of it already—two facts that I doubt will ever change—which is why I'm sure this will work if she'll only hear me out.

"Five grand," I say. I let go of the stack of bills and it thumps to the floor inside her apartment. "Thirty seconds of your time. If you agree, there'll be two extra zeroes on the end of that."

She stops shoving and grunting and leaning on the door long enough to pause and think this over.

Good, I think. *The zebra still has her stripes.*

I feel the pressure ease off the door as she steps back and allows it to slowly swing open.

"Thank you, Kimmie. I'm in something deep and—"

Before I can react, her leg is up in a whip-fast forward kick, burying the top of her foot and those pink-painted toenails into my nads. I let out an *oooph* of pained breath and fall to my knees. I can almost hear her smile around the words as she begins to count, "One, two, three..."

Please allow me to introduce my ex-wife: Kimmie Strand, formerly known as Polly Pettigrew, also known as the Blue Baroness, also known as White Cloud.

I look up, and she's standing there with her arms crossed, hair up in a ponytail, mouth pinched tight in annoyance and anger, looking as tanned, blonde, blue-eyed, and beautiful as ever.

Three years later, she hasn't gotten over the fact that I accepted the NSA contract on her life.

THIRTEEN

Present Day

Eric Landers folds in half like a dishtowel—a small hole in his forehead, bigger hole in the back—and as he goes down, I go with him. It's instinct, and it saves my life. The picture window crackles again and overhead, the untouched bottle of scotch shatters, sending shards of glass and caramel-colored liquid across the wet bar like an alcoholic Rorschach blot.

Given the trajectory, that's a different shooter. A second gunman on higher ground. Doesn't matter—he could be floating in a hot air balloon for all I care—all it means is that there's more than one commando outside, effectively doubling my chances of eating lead before I can get to safety.

Two more shots pepper the glass and I'm not sure what this accomplishes, considering the fact that I'm on the ground and Eric Landers is lying right in front of me, face to face, lifeless and leaking on his pristine hardwood flooring. Maybe there are a couple of the Empire's Storm Troopers out there wasting ammo.

Nah, if that were the case, they wouldn't have hit Landers on the first shot.

Two more bullets rip through the pages of Eric's old law guides on the bookshelves.

Now they're just showing off.

My next thought is poor Dolores upstairs; she has no idea what's happening or that her husband is creating a puddle three floors down. And the kids…their dad, gone, just like that. They're old enough to accept it after a few rounds of therapy, but it sucks losing a parent, no matter what.

Then again, maybe Dolores has an idea of what's happening, because all the way up at the top of the stairs, I hear a frightened, "Who are you? Get out of my—"

Next comes the muted *chuff* of a silencer, followed by an unforgettable gagging sound, then the staccato thump, thump, thump of a body falling three floors, bouncing off the handrails on its way down.

There's another louder, heavier thump right outside the study door, and due to some small bits of lead, the twins are orphaned. Mr. and Mrs. Landers have gone to the great big government building in the sky. I wonder if the lines are as long up there, or if the waiting still feels like an eternity.

Does eternity feel like eternity if you're inside it?

I don't know why my brain processes nonsensical shit like that in the middle of a crisis, but it happens all the time. Truthfully, what I think happens is that the primal sense of instinct kicks into overdrive and works my muscles for me, while the rest of my brain is free to roam.

Point being, I'm pushing myself to my feet, grabbing Eric's long-bladed letter opener off his desk, and shouldering through the study door before I have a chance to consider what's on the other side. It's a good move because the snipers at my back have the window covered. I'm not going that way.

I stay in motion; standing still and peeking down the hallway isn't an option unless I want to feel a bullet pierce my skin. It's been a while since that's happened, and I'm not a fan of the sensation.

I'm counting on the element of surprise because the man, or men, or team on the other side of the door likely expect the both of us to be dead. If I can just get to him before he suspects that the snipers outside were trigger happy, I might have a chance to get out of here alive.

And thank the Good Lord in Heaven it works, because as soon as I'm through, I spook the guy dressed in jet-black tactical gear into inaction. He's wearing a helmet and a set of military grade NVGs, carrying an assault rifle tight against his chest. He's not expecting me, obviously, so it's an easy kill when I stop, drop, and roll, then pop up and deposit the letter opener into his brain from underneath his chin.

He drops like a jacket falling off a clothes hanger, and I'm tempted to go for his weapon because that'd be nice to have on my way out of here. I lean over, reaching, then jerk my hand back when a volley of bullets rips through the body and the floor. The shots come from above, from the one who murdered Dolores.

That's four total, so far.

The dead commando has a small .45 strapped to the side of his leg. It's partially covered from overhead, so I go for that one, snatching it without getting a finger shot off.

I return three shots up the stairwell—not aiming, simply creating a distraction—which works long enough for me to snatch the more powerful assault rifle, dart away from the open area between floors, and sprint head-down toward the entertainment room on the north side of the house.

Think, think, think. What's the layout like out that door? You've been here before, Leo! Think! Okay, garage, pool house. A hedgerow. Senator Michaels lives in the house next door. He gave you that piss-warm beer that time. Stop. Focus. Is there an escape route?

Has to be. They had the back yard covered. Upstairs

covered. Four of them, small tactical team. Two outside, two inside. More than that would be overkill. They'd get in each other's way, right?

I skitter into the entertainment room, slipping on the expensive, unnecessary rug, and then ease the door shut behind me. Not all the way, leaving it open a crack so that I can listen for the sounds of poorly concealed footsteps slinking down the hallway. I can't wait too long because the two jackasses outside will have time to reposition themselves, and the guy upstairs might simply hold his post to give them the opportunity.

I hear nothing.

Son of a bitch.

Either that's exactly what he's doing or he's sneakier than I anticipated.

I have to move. In here, I don't exactly have a ton of room to maneuver. Good vantage points are hard to come by. Sure, I can hide in a closet or under a desk, but I can only guess as to how many goons are out there. Whether it's three or thirty, I'm outnumbered.

Running, slipping into the night, retreating…it's the most logical option, and damn do I hate to run away from a fight, but if the odds are stacked against you, that's how you live to play another day.

I allow myself five more seconds to listen, which

gives me enough time to ponder what this elimination team was doing here in the first place. Did they trail me, or did they already have orders to get rid of Eric Landers, and I happened to be in the way?

Whatever the case, it's not good. For a moment I flip out a little, considering the fact that the head of the NSA and his wife have both been murdered, and I'm inside their house. My fingerprints and DNA are all over the place. My face is probably all over the security cameras. Shit. Well, it'll link one of my identities—not me, specifically—and while that may not lead directly to the capture and arrest of Leo Craft, it's too close for me to be comfortable.

I stop, I breathe, and I consider the fact that there's plenty of evidence to indicate an outside presence was responsible for the murders. Even if they tried to cover their tracks, there's no way they could get someone here to replace the window or, or…

The police. I should call them myself.

The commando team won't expect that. Their total *modus operandi* is to sneak in and out undetected, leaving shattered dreams and cold bodies behind. The question is, do I stick around long enough to keep them distracted until the police arrive?

I don't have time to weigh this decision, because three muffled pops create new holes in the entertainment room door, and since I hadn't closed it all the way, the freaking thing swings open, ever so slowly, allowing my encroacher easy access. I drop low, silently, and crab walk to my right. Outside, in the hallway, a small table rattles, followed by the tinkling of Dolores's curios. I can imagine the bastard cursing himself for being so clumsy.

I scramble behind a love seat and try to hold my breath, because to me, inside my head, I sound like a giant set of bellows huffing at a fire. I hold it until my chest begins to convulse, wondering where he went, or if he chose to abandon this room given his awkward stumble. I take a quick breath, enjoying the sweet release of all that carbon dioxide buildup and the fresh inhalation of oxygen. It's amazing what you take for granted.

Breathing, that perfect engine that keeps the human body—

Chuff, chuff, chuff.

I don't know where those shots went, but they were too close, and he chose poorly.

Head up, arms over the back of the love seat, I find him looking to his left, behind a wall of curtains that have been drawn back from another massive picture window.

I'm kinda old school—valiant, responsible,

chivalrous—so I don't enjoy shooting a man in the back, even when he's trying to kill me. It's a shitty move, one reserved for cowards, cheats, and bastards.

Growing up, I learned many things from Phil, and this was always one of my favorites: go to bed with your dignity intact, because your cereal will taste better in the morning.

I whisper a sharp, "Hey," and the commando whips around.

Pop, pop.

He drops, and I'm on the move again, cell phone in my hand, across the entertainment room the size of Rhode Island.

Okay, that's two internals down. I should be good.

I step around the pool table and note that there's a dart right in the dead center of the bulls-eye hanging on the wall.

Here's a problem I have—I'm hyper aware of things sometimes, especially when I'm in an intense situation, so noticing, and being impressed by the dart in the bulls-eye distracts me from the commando slinking into the entertainment room. I notice too late that he's through the door, assault rifle at the ready against his shoulder.

He fires, and I feel the hot, stinging sensation as the bullet scrapes across the side of my neck.

Oh my God, too close.

I yelp and go down, mostly for theatrics to fool him, and hit the ground harder than I should. It knocks the wind out of me. Next, I'm rolling, rolling underneath the pool table, finger on the trigger, two shots into the kneecaps—*pop, pop*—and he falls to the floor, screaming and holding his legs. His NVGs are resting on top of his helmet, giving me one last look at the surprise in his eyes.

One more bullet is all it takes, and I'm back on my feet, moving, scrambling. I find my cell phone underneath the coffee table. Blood's seeping down my neck, and I can already feel it soaking into the collar of my shirt.

Man, a bullet hasn't grazed my skin in about three years. I'd almost forgotten what it was like.

I pause at the side door to catch my breath. The low valley carved into my neck stings like a son of a bitch.

Be cool, I think. *It'll heal. You're not dead.*

Okay, Leo. Think. Three internals down. Two snipers outside, maybe more. They wouldn't risk approaching across the lawn with the floodlights and the moon. Smartest approach would be…what? Flanking the house if they're trying to enter? North, south. Right? So that leaves possibly one more to go before I can—how much ammo do I have left?

For the first time since I picked it up, I look closely at the assault rifle in my hands. Before I can eject the clip to take stock of my remaining rounds, something on the side of the stock catches my attention: a SALCON insignia.

Fourteen

Two Weeks Earlier, Con't.

Kimmie listens to what I have to say, then sits back against her couch, speechless, as she props her head up against a hand. Cotton candy pink fingernails cap off a set of long, luxurious fingers; the very same fingers that used to give me the best damn massages a guy could ask for.

The good news is, she's got a smile on her face. The bad news is, it's a devious sort of grin that's full of "I told you so" and smug satisfaction.

She pulls her legs underneath her on the couch, and I can't help but look at how muscular, but feminine, her legs are. She's held onto her White Cloud shape when she could've easily stopped the genetically modified injections that made her a superhero to begin with. She says, "I've actually dreamed about this moment for a while now. And you're seriously going to go through with it?"

I break eye contact and stare out the window at the hummingbird flitting near the feeder. There's too much glee in her gaze to keep looking at her. I offer an accepting nod. "It's time, I think."

"After what you did to me, Leo, it's *beyond* time."

Okay, so long story short, Polly Pettigrew and I were married and for all intents and purposes, it was fantastic—for a while. We both led very different lives, as can be imagined, but it worked, and it worked well for *us*. I loved her with every molecule of my being when she was the Blue Baroness (Get it? Oil baron's daughter?), and I thought that nothing could ever come between us. We'd bought a house outside of Houston and were even considering an attempt at a little Leo or Polly.

Then, one day, I walk into her dad's office, unannounced, and find her cutting oil shipment deals with some members of the Chinese government. She was already worth billions, at least on paper, but more never hurt…until it did. I knew that if some of the upper level suits running this fine country ever found out what she was up to they'd take my dear heart away. There were arguments and long nights of discussions, and she promised she'd stop, so we paid off some no-name supervillain, a guy that went by Starbreaker, to participate in this epic battle in the middle of Times Square.

He won as planned, the Blue Baroness "died" from her wounds en route to the hospital, and everything was hunky dory with Polly and me for a while. At least until I left for a conference in Vegas one weekend, and by the time I got back, she'd resurrected herself as White Cloud.

At the time, I huffed, sighed, and let it go because happy wife, happy life, right? A month later, she was back to cutting deals with foreign governments to ship her father's oil for marked-up wholesale prices that were still cheaper than what they could get through international trade.

Anyway, all that boring crap out of the way, the second time around, I absolutely could not convince her that she needed to stop, so I found out through a number of different channels—mostly Phil—that the United States government had marked her.

I made some calls, took the contract, and forced her into yet another retirement because in the eyes of the NSA, she was dead by my hands. The Blue Baroness had been reincarnated as White Cloud and died again; Polly Pettigrew had been reincarnated as Kimmie Strand, who was alive...and not very thankful for it.

Since she was so fond of money, and spending it, and doing so while she was breathing, she flipped me the bird, and true to form, delivered a sharp kick to the crotch, then left me moaning beside the toilet in our old house.

These days, she maintains a low profile, spending her time travelling around the world, keeping her tan even, drinking boat drinks, and hating my guts.

All in all, I'd say she leads a pretty good life. The genetic modifications she pays a hundred grand for on a monthly basis via some shadow company barely puts a dent in her bank account, and they leave her with an amazing body that she doesn't have to work hard at to keep. Cheeseburgers? Two of them, please! A whole pizza? Why not!

My ex-wife…tanned, toned, and terribly vindictive.

Gorgeous, but I have to be careful, because I'm not convinced that she wouldn't choke me to death if I take my eyes off her.

Kimmie jams a finger into my chest and repeats herself, "It's *beyond* time."

I push her finger away, and not gently. "I know, and we can go around and around, again—"

She tosses her hands in the air and says, "And it was the *only* way to save my life," as she rolls her eyes. "Song and dance, Leo."

I readjust myself on the couch; one, to keep a better eye on her, and two, I'm getting myself into a position to break for the door if she decides to go ballistic on me. I'm getting the feeling that she hasn't softened a bit in three years. This might've been one of the worst ideas I've ever had. "Just hear me out, okay? If we're gonna do this, we need to be at the airport in, like, thirty minutes."

"Tell me again."

"Okay, well, not that you'll be the one to kill Patriotman, per se, but here's what I'm thinking. And seriously, Polly—"

"*Kimmie*," she reminds me. She points at her chest. "Don't forget you made this."

"Right, sorry. Regardless, it's your chance for redemption, revenge, whatever."

"If I'm not the one to kill Patriotman, how does that benefit me again?"

I explain my plan to her, and truthfully, I get a little choked up. She knows how much this means to me. She also knows how well I can read a person's micro-expressions, so she holds her face flat and unmoving, like a beautiful blonde statue carved from tanned…things.

When I finish, she says, "And that's how you plan to resurrect me? I've supposedly been alive for three years, living in some tropical place as Patriotman's glorified love slave?"

"Yup." It's all I've got.

"White Cloud comes back to track down Patriotman's murderer?

"Yup." I wait. It's all I can do.

"Leo?"

"Yeah?"

"I don't know if you're an idiot or a goddamn genius." She's up from the couch and moving toward her bedroom. Admittedly, I admire the taut, not-so-subtle curves underneath the thin sweatpants material. "Stop staring at my ass," she says over her shoulder.

"Sorry."

"No, you're not," she calls to me from inside her closet that's bigger than my bedroom. "Fix some coffee while I pack."

"So you're coming?"

"If you screw me on this, I'll castrate you."

"But then you won't have anything left to kick."

"Just make the damn coffee, Leo. And call Daddy. Tell him I said we're taking the private jet. There's no way I'm flying to the Maldives on a commercial airplane. You should know better than that."

I grin and rummage through the cabinets. "Yes, ma'am."

This might just work after all. It's something I've been thinking about for a long time.

***

Tennyson Pettigrew—a "lord" in his own mind—meets us at the Houston airport where all the private jets are located. Ordinarily, he wouldn't be bothered to come down off his high perch atop one of the largest high-rises in the city. Pettigrew Oil Services is, at its foundation, a one-stop shop for anything the roughnecks and roustabouts, company men and drillers, could need out in the field. Some of his elders started out in a garage—go figure—about a hundred and twenty years ago, selling drill bits they'd designed and built themselves. They were eons ahead of their time, and the money flowed into their coffers like…well, like oil from a gusher.

Next thing you know, a century and change later, POS—hah, guess what I say it stands for?—brings in approximately forty-five billion dollars in annual revenue. Pettigrew himself is worth about twenty-seven billion, and that's if you only count what's publicly accessible. I almost got Kimmie to tell me one time, but the only thing she'd say was, "Daddy could buy Bill Gates' entire fortune and still have enough left over to afford the Yankees' salary."

So, yeah. Dude's rich.

And he hates my guts. Like father, like daughter.

Always has, even before I unofficially murdered his little girl for the NSA. It's not like I was an underachiever in his eyes. Matter of fact, I was far from it, ask anybody you know, but for most fathers, the scumbag trying to get in his daughter's panties wasn't worth his weight in dog shit.

I figure he's here to voice his displeasure over our trip together, but Kimmie's a big girl now. He can't tell her what to do, so *nyah, nyah, nyah.*

We're standing outside the white LearJet with the Pettigrew company logo painted on the tail—a large, blue P with a stem that looks like a downhole drill bit, encased in a piss-yellow circle—waiting on the crew to finish readying the plane for our departure.

They're all scrambling, from the pilot and co-pilot, to the flight attendant, to the mechanic and grounds crew, because this is an unscheduled trip. They're used to Daddy Oilbucks having trips arranged days, weeks, and months in advance, but what Daughter Dearest says goes as well, so here we are, thumb-twiddling until they call us on board.

We could be inside the damn thing, drinking champagne already, but Kimmie insisted on waiting in the hangar for the *paterfamilias*, who, from the looks of it, is ready to spit bullets at my head. He probably could, too.

It has to be said: Tennyson Pettigrew is a juggernaut of a man. Broad shoulders, about as wide as a dumpster, with a head like a watermelon sitting between them. I don't mean to say that he's green with stripes, just that the dude doesn't have a neck and his head is sort of rounded off into a point. Some people eat Grape Nuts for breakfast, Old Man Pettigrew probably fills his cereal bowl with diamonds and whole milk. And damn, is he ever strong. He lifts, daily, and chows down something like eight thousand calories—no lie—and barely has an ounce of fat on him.

How he finds time to run a multinational corporation with thirty-five thousand employees and still lift like Schwarzenegger as if it's a full-time job is beyond me. Maybe he doesn't have to. Maybe it's natural. There are rumors that he ran with the Incredible Hulk back in the 70s; could you imagine the two of them raging out together, having pillow fights with tanks? There's no proof of him as a superhero, however, except for a handful of grainy photographs. I figure that's where Kimmie got her ideas about life as a genetically altered badass.

Anyway, point is, the dude has everything going for him. Billions of dollars, body like two of me put together, a gorgeous, debutante daughter that used to be universally loved until her fall from grace—because what family doesn't have a black sheep—and a smartass former son-in-law that's just as handsome today as he was yesterday…what more could the guy want?

Me, dead and gone, apparently. Guess I was wrong.

This is the first time I've seen him since I sent his little girl, a.k.a. White Cloud, to her grave, and from what I can tell, there are a lot of unresolved issues.

I don't know why he's so mad—he knows I didn't kill her because she's standing right beside me, but he's charging forward like an Angus bull on amphetamines, and I'm fairly sure I can see steam coming out of his ears.

He's about fifty feet away, yet I can see the red hue in his cheeks getting darker.

"What's his problem?" I ask.

Kimmie crosses her arms and chuckles. "You killed me."

"I most certainly did not."

"It's the thought that counts, Leo."

"I *never* had any intention of going through with it. You know that, and he knows that. It's your own damn fault that the feds caught onto your—your shenanigans, not once, but twice, may I remind you, and, *and*, I'm pretty sure I did you a favor by letting them think you're dead."

She grins and flicks her chin toward her father. "Explain that to him."

How can she get by with some people, like the flight crew, knowing that she's still alive while the government thinks she's dead and buried by my hands? Easy, they're more terrified of Tennyson Pettigrew than they are of Uncle Sam. Right about now, I might be, too.

"I thought it was…right."

She pinches my cheek and makes mushy, baby-face noises, then adds, "Doesn't matter, Smoochykins. You never mess with Daddy's little girl."

Tennyson Pettigrew gets to within five feet of me, arms out, blood boiling, hands grasping like a pissed off crab—his face is about the color of one, too—and he says, "Come 'ere, you little bastard."

I react the only way I know how.

I lower myself to dodge his grasp, grab him around the waist, and then I throw him roughly thirty yards distant, where he lands in pile of boxes marked *FluffyTime Pillows*. I imagine they were a shipment waiting to go out, and lucky for him, they were there.

"Leo!" Kimmie scolds me. "Did you *have* to do that?"

Fifteen

Present Day

When my heart drops out of my throat long enough for me to take a breath, I blink and focus again to reassure myself. Yep, that's a damn SALCON insignia engraved into the side of the barrel. Ironically enough, it's a large, fat *S* inside a diamond shape with a dove at the eastern point and an olive branch opposite of that. *Peace* symbols, and here I am, looking at a dead guy and the instrument that caused it.

Peace my ass.

Seriously, can the shit get any deeper? A SALCON commando team taking out the head of the NSA? If anything makes sense in this godforsaken ordeal, that's the one thing that does. SALCON is the united front of superheroes and they're probably not happy that someone has been giving orders to off their members.

I wouldn't be, obviously.

I slink over to the side door that looks out toward their driveway on the side of the house. I don't know why it's even there, considering the five-car garage on the front side leaves plenty of room for Dolores's scooter collection. The top half of the door is paned glass, and a nearby streetlamp gives me enough light to survey the territory. I don't see any SALCON commandos coming up or down the driveway where green moss and small, leafy weeds sprout up among the bricks. A fat, thick, impenetrable hedgerow creates a solid boundary between the two property lines, so there's no way I'm cutting across.

Looks to be all clear. My car is two blocks over, to the east, parked next to another multi-million dollar mansion that probably houses a chubby, white-haired leader of whatever subcommittee he was able to wrangle control of. Or maybe he's a foreign NATO rep here on U.S. soil. Or maybe he's even a retired SALCON heavy.

As I've said, SALCON is sort of like the U.N. or NATO of the tights and muscles crowd, a global representative organization that fights for the rights of those who keep the world a safer place, but who aren't often accepted into normal society because of their special abilities.

Look at it this way: it's a governing body for the freaks of the planet.

The leader is a guy with white hair and a white goatee, aptly named The Minion. Not quite a superhero name that strikes fear in the heart of morons, but the dude is a genius and a perfect figurehead capable of matching wits with foreign and domestic politicians.

The fact that SALCON is here, and that they've eliminated Eric Landers, makes perfect sense because it's likely that someone finally found out that he was one of the three American upper-level suits calling in orders to eliminate SALCON underlings and superheroes all around the world for the past three years. There are plenty of foreign leaders placing orders, too, but the U.S. is by far the biggest proprietor of our services.

It would be like Kofi Annan, that awesome guy from the U.N., finding out that former President George Bush had been using the NSA, CIA, and FBI to employ elite assassins to eliminate marks with close ties to the U.N. council—then, Kofi gets pissed and fights back.

Which means, in all sincerity, that Conner Carson and Joe Gaylord, the top dogs of the FBI and CIA, are probably already dead, dying, or marked for elimination, so there goes my ability to extract more information that they possibly didn't have. I'm not going to risk approaching them now, not a chance in hell. If I show up at either one of their houses, I could easily have a red dot centered on *my* forehead.

In fact, I don't have the slightest clue what my next move should be.

All I know is, I gotta get somewhere and process all this.

I step out of the side door and quickly scan up and down the side of the house. It's chilly outside, and I can feel the low-hanging fog speckling against my cheeks.

I drop beside a garbage can that smells like rotten chicken and take another look.

Nothing going on, all clear. I can only guess where the two snipers at the backside of the house went, but I'm in a spot where they can't get a good shot at me, regardless. So, what I do is, I back up to the hedgerow—to get out of the bright glow of the streetlight—and I slink sideways for what feels like miles. Eric Landers has…*had*…a humongous house.

Had. I shake my head. He was a great guy, and it's still too soon to think of him in the past tense.

When I reach the street, I pause for a moment, surveying the neighborhood, and my senses fully process what's going on around me. I pick up on the mossy, wet smell of the landscaped and coiffed yards. A slight breeze pushes maples and pines to the side like old friends giving a shoulder a nudge. Somewhere a dog barks, and behind me, Eric and Dolores are dead in their home, due to a SALCON attack that I never saw coming.

I move. I need to get to a safer place. This is all too much new information to analyze while I'm on the run.

As if things weren't screwed up enough.

I put one foot in front of the other, walking in a hurry, trying to keep my head down and not attract attention. My shoes are soft-soled rubber but every subtle step sounds like a bunker buster taking out some Taliban stronghold.

This is a neighborhood where some insomniac would definitely notice an interloper bleeding from a superficial wound in his neck at almost four a.m., but what do you do? It's chancy to walk quietly and calmly because I still run the risk of taking a bullet to the head, but my gut's telling me those snipers are long gone. Have to be. If they'd tried to radio their comrades inside the home and no one responded, then undoubtedly they weren't prepared for an entity who would put up a fight against their trained commandos. My guess is they'd confirmed the death of Eric Landers then retreated to report back to SALCON.

There had also been rumors among the members of SASS that SALCON was working on something big, and we all thought they were planning to hit the

Japanese because they'd been so vocal in their disagreements with SALCON's political wrangling as of late.

Nobody within SASS knew a damn inkling of truth, and I had no reason to be suspicious of any of them. All I was supposed to do is figure out which one of them is plotting an attempt on Palmer's life, which had absolutely nothing to do with SALCON or their movements.

Which also makes me wonder, if they know who had been barking the orders, do they know who had been doing the dirty deeds?

If that's the case, that's big. Too big. That means they're coming after me, my friends, and God, I hope not, but my family is a possibility, too.

Am I in danger? is a rhetorical question, because I'm always in danger, but what about the other members of SASS? Charlene? John Conklin, Don Weiss, the Charlies, Tara and Mara, and the rest of the crew?

Dallas, I'm not so worried about her. You know…just because.

Are the hunters becoming the hunted?

Do I have time to warn them all? Should I waste the time? They're highly trained assassins who can hold their own.

Self-preservation, man. You gotta go. Now.

No, wait. The phone tree, remember? Who was first? Charlene?

Call her, let it go down the line. One call, Leo. One and done. That's why it's called a support group, dumbass. For support.

I lift my phone to dial then think better of it. I'd momentarily forgotten that Charlene knew more about my current status with DPS than she should've.

I can still trust *her*, can't I?

That's a tough one, and right now, I'm in such deep crap that it feels like a brontosaurus took a dump on me, and I can't afford another what-if scenario. Okay, so I'm not calling Charlene, definitely not Dallas, which leaves me nine choices. Maybe, just maybe, I'm unintentionally crying wolf here, and SALCON doesn't know who did the dirty work, only who was in charge, but something tells me that if they were able to infiltrate the government enough to find out who did the hiring, then you better believe they know who the underlings are.

Makes sense, doesn't it?

And, if I call and get the phone tree going, that might alert the culprit that his cover is blown, and I'll have no chance of catching Palmer's attempted murderer.

I guess the question now is, do I even care?

As I walk, pondering, trying to pull the pieces together, I'm about a half block away from my rental car when I pass a large mansion with a white stone façade on the side facing the street. Lush green vines creep up the trellises, and it's pitch dark inside.

An unholy conglomeration of nature that looks to be a crossbred Corgi and Beagle pitter-pats down the walkway and stops behind his master's wrought-iron fence. He fires a small grumble at me, nothing more than a warning shot across the bow, and then retreats back up toward his porch, toenails clicking like a typewriter.

It's not until his ears perk up, and he flashes a quick look over his shoulder that I realize someone is behind me.

My stomach muscles clench and I hesitate, processing the situation. SALCON commandos would've shot me dead already. Anybody with trailing tactics capable enough to get that close, without me noticing, would've either pulled the trigger, slid a knife into my ribs, or tightened the garrote wire, so it's likely not someone who wants me dead. And I'm making this guess purely by default.

Still I can't risk anything, so I spin around, duck low, and get ready to pounce.

I brought along one of the dead commando's

Smith & Wesson .45, and it's pointing directly at the head of—

"Deke? What the hell?" I stand up.

He drops his hands once he realizes I'm not going to shoot him in the face.

Honestly, I would've expected to see Santa Claus kissing Elvis before I could've anticipated Deke Carter trailing me through an upscale neighborhood in northern Virginia at four o'clock in the morning.

He glances at my neck. "Jesus, Leo, you okay?"

"What're you doing here, man? I almost shot you." My frustration is palpable, and he backs up a step. His white, fluffy hair isn't as pristinely plastered against his head as it usually is, and his light blue suit and white collared shirt look rumpled, as if he's had a long, hard day. Right now, I'm not conjuring up much sympathy for him.

"I should ask you the same thing," Deke says. Granted, I have the .45 in my hand, and his weapon remains tucked squarely away in his shoulder holster, but he's showing no signs of being here as an arresting authority. Maybe he doesn't know anything about what happened back at Eric's place.

"Do you have a car nearby?"

"Yeah, it's parked right behind yours."

"Then let's go." I flash my eyes up and down the

street, looking for any signs of approaching SALCON grunts and spot nothing out of the ordinary. About six blocks down, an absurdly early morning jogger wearing a yellow reflective vest passes by on a cross street, but that's it.

"What were you doing with Eric Landers?" Deke asks.

"Baking cookies." I grab his arm and drag him with me. He doesn't resist. It seems silly, though, like I'm punishing a seventy-year-old man as if he's a toddler, so I let go, and thankfully he follows like a good little boy. We cross the quiet street, and I repeat my question. "What're you doing here? Trailing me? Spying? What?"

"Agent Kelly asked me to follow you once you left Portland."

"And how, exactly, did you manage to do that? I'd never used that ID before. It was brand new."

Deke flicks a grin at me as he's removing his car keys from a pants pocket. "We have ways."

"Nope!" I hold up a finger like I'm scolding him. "Nope, nope. Not playing that game, Deke. If you have no clue what's going on, and I'm assuming you don't, because you would've said something if you did… This is deeper than me, you, Lisa Kelly…everybody involved, and I'm not about to play

Pin the Tail on the Dumbass with you. Give me the keys and tell me how."

"The GPS on your phone, dummy. It's about as easy as watching you on a video monitor."

I…I don't have anything to say to that. Point goes to Deke, because that had totally slipped my mind.

We reach a white Ford sedan—a rental that's way nicer than mine—and Deke reluctantly tosses the keys to me.

"Get in the car."

Chirp-chirp. The doors unlock.

"What were you doing with Eric Landers?"

"Watching a bunch of SALCON commandos put a bullet between his eyes."

Deke pauses, chuckles like I'm joking, and then his eyes go wide when I don't return his smile.

SIXTEEN

Two Weeks Earlier, Con't.

Okay, well, now…hang on a minute before any of those proverbial conclusions are jumped to, let me explain. I never said a word about being an average guy on the street. There may have been a few details I left out, however.

A few big ones, no doubt, but a guy has to have some secrets.

It's true: I am the hero known as Patriotman, masquerading as Leo Craft the assassin.

Why?

Why…*everything?*

That's a good question.

I spent my entire goddamn life hiding my true identity as a superhuman. From the moment I came out of my mother like I was riding a Slip n' Slide on a hot July day, sick, weak, and diseased to the point of nearly dying on the operating table, I've been…special. For the first ten years of my life, there were cold labs, needles that injected warm fluid in my body—fluids that no other human on the planet has used or ever will use again—along with beeping monitors and lumpy hospital beds.

Underground laboratories, government officials in dark suits and darker sunglasses, and those late night knocks on the door, only to be whisked away from dear old Mom and Dad for another round of testing. Was I progressing well? Were my muscles developing at the predetermined rate that had been programmed into the live microbial cells swimming around in my weekly injections? What was my sperm count like? Was I behaving like a normal teenager? Crusty socks, hormones raging whenever I saw a cute girl in short shorts?

Yes, yes, and yes.

Great, we have big plans for you.

How it all went down is another story altogether, but I will say this, the men who made me are no longer with us, so that only the people I chose would ever learn my secrets, and to assuage my guilt I spent three decades as America's Hero, the Defender of the Human Race, Friend of Planet Earth, God Among Men, the Elite of Elites—whatever. All that shit still makes me sick to my stomach.

It's how I met Polly, it's how I tossed Tennyson Pettigrew like a stubby-necked softball, and it's how I knew that George Silver was lying about Patriotman turning his back on the American people in order to join the North Koreans. That's when I knew something was up.

I don't doubt for one second that there's someone plotting to kill President Palmer, and it very well may be someone within SASS, but believe me when I say that I have never been approached by an assassin, nor did I attempt to turn someone against the leader of the free world like George Silver's crocodile tears tried to lay testament to.

I believe this to be true because I hear things when I'm out and about. Chatter across the wires, if you will. When you're involved in a profession like mine, the new one, it's difficult to not get caught up in all the crazy shit that Joe Six-Pack would never suspect.

I didn't—and don't—have any specific details. It could be one of seven billion people plotting to murder Palmer, but it ain't me. I also believe this because of Agent Kelly and Deke Carter's total surprise at George Silver's presence at the black site during our last visit.

Unless she was lying, and I didn't pick up on that at all, she'd confirmed with her superiors that Silver did indeed own the wallet that funded Direct Protection Services, but he had no hand in the day-to-day operations, not typically, and his request to eliminate Patriotman had nothing to do with my mission to uncover the president's potential assailant.

There are so many things that don't make sense to me right now that I couldn't even begin to guess which one of them makes the *least* sense, but one of the highest ones on the list is, why exactly does George Silver, the Secretary of Defense, want Patriotman dead? I suspect that he plans to publicly blame me, the *Patriotman* me, for whatever's going to happen—or is supposed to happen—to President Palmer, but why me? There are literally dozens of superheroes out there working that could be the patsy.

That's the reason for the setup with Kimmie. I figure that if I give her a chance to see my alternate identity die, and then resurrect herself as a brand new heroine, I'm doing double duty. I'm giving her an opportunity to forgive me, and I'm *completely* freeing myself of that godforsaken identity so that I can uncover Silver's true intentions.

Now for the confusing part: I got sick of the double-standard, double-sided, double-crossing nature of so many of my fellow "heroes" that I could no longer feel proud of the work we were doing for humanity. I'm semi-retired as Patriotman, and occasionally I'll show up to thwart some bank robbery or hostage situation to keep the persona fresh in the public eye.

Outside of that, I have a guy—in the Maldives, lucky bastard—who looks so much like me that my own mother would get confused. His name is Bart Alonzo, and he earns his living as my stand-in *doppelganger.* The funny thing is, he looks *exactly* like me, like my minute-apart identical twin, but it doesn't make a damn bit of difference because nobody has ever seen Patriotman's face. If he ever makes an appearance as me, he's behind the mask. When I ran into him in Barcelona one sunny afternoon a few years ago, I hired him on the spot because it was so uncanny. I figured if I ever needed to have my face shown, it might be good to have a stunt double, just in case.

Sadly for Bart, in another couple of days, he'll be out of a job.

Mostly what I do now is eliminate the sons-of-bitches who don't deserve to be adored by fans the world over.

You think Billie Bombshell is all puppy dogs and roses with her pretty smile and, admittedly, perfectly glorious bottom in that set of blue tights? Underneath that mask is a brutally evil home-wrecker who has ruined more marriages than Monday Night Football. Behind that smile is an alcoholic nymphomaniac who couldn't care less about the people she's trying to save. As long as there's a penis and a bottle of whiskey handy, she'll fight crime all day.

And what about the Scarlett Gargoyle? He was no better. That guy was running a prostitution ring with rich, white Wall Street guys as clients and fourteen-year-old Vietnamese girls as the chattel. Disgusting. On the side, he fought crime in a bright red outfit with a chartreuse-colored lightning bolt down the sides of his legs.

Or the *Crimson* Gargoyle? The cheap, knockoff, poor man's copycat who fancied himself just as good as his slightly more vibrant counterpart. I took that contract without wavering for a millisecond because nothing could've pleased me more than to watch that cocaine smuggler burn. (Not literally. He died when I released an air bubble into his jugular vein.) Who knows how many lives he ruined when he enlisted the help of underage thugs in South Central L.A. to help him move his product.

What is it with the Gargoyles and kids, huh?

Sam Diamond—I swore I'd never talk about that guy again, but here goes: we served together in Desert Storm. Mainly we were over there as figureheads, almost like a Bob Hope USO kind of thing, to lift morale for the troops. It's not as if we couldn't have fought ourselves, and damn, we volunteered for a few missions, but the upper-level generals said absolutely not. It's like how NFL coaches barely play their stars during pre-season; you don't want them to get hurt.

Anyway, Sam wouldn't take no for an answer, and three days later, we found him in the center of a smoldering village, eating the fresh heart of a puppy while the innocent Iraqi citizens bloated and festered in the summer heat.

He denied that it was him, but two things gave him away: the puppy heart, for one, and two, that particular village had been under surveillance for about six weeks. The local commanding officers in that region had a guy under cover—he didn't make it. The camera mounted in his shawl did.

Let me say this… Sam Diamond deserved what I gave him. I'm not ashamed of it, and part of me is ticked that I waited so long to do it, because who knows what other atrocities that sick fucker committed on the rest of humanity, all while he smiled for the cameras, wore red, white, and blue, and saluted our fallen heroes after yet another victorious battle against some no-name supervillain.

To sum up, after I made the decision to help out when the good guys weren't so good, I jumped at the chance when the Prime Minister of Australia called me personally to place an order.

Don't get me wrong, not everyone doing battle for the right is really evil deep down. Some of them simply have a darker side that their adoring public never gets to see.

Even heroes wear masks.

If some of the people wearing white hats have black hearts, why fight for the good guys?

That's easy. The perks are better.

If you're an asshole supervillain, you might be able to take what you want, like girls, guns, and money. That's great—you're living like a mad king and loving every second of it—until you realize that all the white knights in town are vying to be the first one to bury you and claim the reward. You can only exist as a supervillain for so long before some schmuck like Captain Kane comes along and makes a name for himself at your expense.

That's probably why most of them hang out on private islands with nigh impenetrable fortresses. It'd say it's a bit like Tom Cruise hiding from the paparazzi, but instead of cameras flashing in your face the moment you step into the sunlight, it's fists, roundhouse kicks, and fancy gadgets shooting laser beams at your face.

The smart ones will strap on an American flag like a cape, fire off a few BAMs, BIFFs, and POWs, put a couple of criminals behind bars, then enjoy free drinks on the house until the adoration starts to wane. Walk into the middle of the biggest art heist in New York's history, announce yourself as Billy Barbell, take down some punks, and then bite chunks of flesh out of unsuspecting hookers, nobody will ever be the wiser while you gladly accept bottles of champagne and the key to the city.

It disgusted me, and I couldn't take it anymore. It sickened me so much that I felt fake, that I felt like my heart wasn't pure, that it was tainted for knowing these things and letting them go. I justified it by thinking, "Hey, they're helping the human race, so what if he chewed off that girl's nipple?" I understand how bad that sounds, but is it worth turning a blind eye to someone who commits atrocities as long as he's still doing good on the surface?

What about the televangelist who gives hope to millions and then snorts a five-pound bag of coke out of a stripper's ass crack, then goes on a rampage and kills her in his hotel room?

Or what about the pro baseball outfielder earning a hundred and forty million dollars over ten seasons; can we forgive him of that fatal hit and run as long as he continues to help build homes in Guatemala during the off season?

I felt sleazy by association.

So much falsity hidden under the banner of good intentions.

That's when I went on *Tonight with Don Donner*, announced my semi-retirement to the listening world, to much wailing and gnashing of teeth, and then walked off the set.

Five people in the world know that I'm Patriotman. Clark Kent, Bart Alonzo, Mom, Phil, and Polly…er…Kimmie. White Cloud, Blue Baroness, whatever, which is an amazing surprise considering she's kept that secret all this time.

Not counting the two ex-girlfriends who ran for their lives after I explained what I did for a living, three people know that I assassinate superheroes: Mom, Phil, and Kimmie.

And it's true; I do it for the greater good because I'm not built to do anything else. It's a job with a purpose. I could walk away from superherodom for good and let someone else worry about it. I could get a job and be a good citizen, but let me say this… I'd die in a cube. I'd die behind the wheel of a pizza delivery van. I'd die selling cars.

Not literally, but my soul would.

While some of my colleagues disgusted me so much that I had to take a break from it all, I don't pick and choose, though some days I'd like to. That's between God and the government they pissed off. My employers and my maker are the judge and the jury.

I'm the Executioner.

Funny. Too bad that name is already taken.

SEVENTEEN

Present Day

Deke leans back in his seat and puts a wrinkled, liver-spotted hand on his forehead. It's shaking like a Chihuahua in winter, and he asks, somberly, "Landers is dead?"

"Yep." I throw his rental car into reverse, back it up a nudge, and then leave mine behind. Somebody will find it eventually, and that fake bank account has enough in it to cover whatever overdue charges might be coming my way. I'm like that, see, worried about being a good guy even when there are much, much bigger things happening that I need to concentrate on.

"Holy shit."

"Holy shit is right, and I need you to listen to me, Deke. I need you to tell me everything you know about this goddamn case. I want to know why George Silver wanted Patriotman dead, I want to know why you guys think that one of the S.A.'s in SASS is plotting to kill Palmer and if that's even a real thing, and above all else, you wrinkled old ball-sack, I want to know why in the immortal fuck a SALCON commando team wanted Eric Landers dead. And before you say a

-185-

fucking word, you better goddamn believe that I deserve the truth, because I'm sick of playing your little errand boy. I could've died back there, and Eric and his wife didn't deserve to."

Deke sighs through his nose while I check the mirrors. No tails. We're in the clear as far as I can tell.

"Well?"

"It, uh… It gets worse, Leo." The tone in his voice is so downtrodden that I can't fathom a guess as to what's coming next.

"How, Deke? How can it possibly get worse?"

"I don't like being the one to tell you this, but it's better that you learn now—"

I punch the dashboard. An air vent crumbles and falls out of its slot. "Learn…*what?*"

"They, um, they found…" He clears his throat and I swear, I'm within an inch of punching *him* instead of the dashboard if he doesn't hurry up. "They found Phil."

My stomach drops a little. "What does that mean? You mean, like, found him walking down the street in his pajamas? Found him at the casino?" I have an inkling of what he's about to say, but son of a bitch, I'm trying hard to pretend like it's not true.

"No, uh…double tap to his chest. Two clean wounds and the locals are running ballistics on the bullets now. Luckily, or maybe not so much… He was on the phone with your mom when it happened. She says they were talking about you, and then he just went silent. If she hadn't been talking to him, he might still be there."

I've been hit by a lot of things. Supervillains that can swing anvils like boxing gloves. This mammoth bastard named, well, Mammoth, who could use a light pole as if it was a thirty-two-ounce Louisville Slugger. Hell, I've even been hit by a few speeding trains and I once had a shell from a tank slam into my shield so hard that it took the wind out of me for a good fifteen minutes. I've been bruised, battered, and had my chest pounded on with cinderblocks by a real badass nasty named She-Beast.

But nothing, nothing, has ever hit me harder than hearing that The Oracle, Phil, my father and buddy, is dead.

I haven't cried in thirty-five years and damn it, I'm not about to start now, but this hurts, bad. My chest heaves. My eyes are watering. I've bitten my bottom lip so hard that I can taste the subtle, metallic hint of blood.

That same, bloody lip starts to quiver, and I don't know how I'm driving like this. My body can't contain this emotion. My chest is on fire. My legs and arms burn, craving action, any kind of release. I want to kick down brick walls with my bare feet. I want to crush marble statues in my fists. I want to spit acid. I want to grind anything good into a fine mist underneath my bleeding knuckles.

For the first time ever, I think I can truly understand how some people become evil.

I want revenge.

And nothing will stand in my way until I get it.

But first, I need answers.

I grind my teeth together. I could chew through Wolverine's adamantium claws. "Who?" I growl.

Deke shakes his head. "They don't know yet."

"Bullshit."

"Look, I'm sorry—"

"Yeah, right."

"Honest to God. I know it hurts, but you know how it works, Leo. Still too early in the game. The two guys running the case, a guy named DiMarco and one named Bailey, they're good, and right now they're tagging the scene, and they've put a rush on the ballistics. Lisa's there, too."

"I thought you guys stayed in the shadows? You're sweepers, aren't you?"

"She's flashing FBI creds for now, trying to throw them off. We were paying attention to you when it came across the wire. Otherwise, we'd might've been there soon enough to shut it down. Now it'll be up to Homicide because we can't run the risk of blowing our cover to pull rank on them."

It hits me again. Phil is dead. My dad is dead. "Fuck!" I punch the steering wheel. I try to pull up, but even my light touch bends it. I quickly change the subject because Deke doesn't know my true identity. I have to keep him talking.

Pull your shit together, Leo. Stable now, mourn later.

"What does Agent Kelly think?" I feel a tear building at the corner of my eye. I rub at my face with a sleeve to disguise the fact that I'm wiping it away before it falls.

"From the looks of it, she says it's a clean elimination. Professional. Given what went on back there at the Landers place, I'm inclined to believe it might be a well-orchestrated SALCON hit, but I'd need to call Lisa to discuss it. That's the only thing that indicates a professional job except…" He almost continues, then catches himself.

"That what?"

"They found a long red hair."

"So? Dad, er, *Phil* had all kinds of girlfriends. Or hookers, or strippers. Could've been the pizza delivery girl."

"I'm only suggesting…"

"Oh, I know what you're suggesting, and it sounds like total horseshit to me. Charlene? *Charlene?* Are you kidding me? She works with the DPS, doesn't she? She's on our side, right? Nope, not a chance, Deke. Not unless…" That flicker in the back of my mind becomes a flashing distress beacon. I whip the car into an empty spot along the sidewalk. It's quiet still, but early enough that some lights are coming on. Early morning risers trying to beat the insanity of the northern Virginia commute. "It's a stretch, but what if *Dallas* planted the red hair?"

Deke shrugs. "I'm not going to say yes to that, because anything's possible, but Leo, c'mon, she was removed from DPS two months ago. She's got no knowledge of any inner workings."

"That doesn't mean that she's not a puppet for someone else outside of the organization. Jesus, it's starting to make sense, isn't it?"

"How so?"

"Give me a sec." I see that the windows are fogging up from our body heat inside and the cool, moist temperatures outside. If we were followed, it's a disadvantage to us without being able to spot someone on the approach, but at the same time, it'll be good to hide ourselves as targets while I process this.

Phil is lingering there in the back of my mind, blocking clear thought processes, and I can feel that lump in my throat, refusing to go away. I swallow, hard, and say a small prayer to the roof of Deke's rental car.

Dad…damn it. Yes, Dad. *I love you, and I'm sorry I wasn't there to protect you. You stepped up when you didn't have to. You helped, you cared, and you were around. You were a good man. So good. You couldn't keep your dick in your pants around Mom, and she was never enough for you, not by herself, but you loved her in your own dumbass way, and I can't fault you for that, I guess. We'll talk about this later, but for right now, I gotta get shit done, man. I love you, I'll miss you, and I'll see you on the other side.*

I picture hanging up the phone to the afterlife in my imagination, and that helps clear my mind a little, helps me focus on the present. I can do nothing for Phil at this very moment—Agent Kelly is there to ask questions—so it's my job to solve this whole goddamn thing, which, in turn, will avenge Phil's death.

A long red hair, huh? Whether it was Charlene, Dallas, or that comedian, Carrot Top, or someone entirely different…it's time to pay the Patriot.

Deke fidgets in his seat and clears his throat. Leaning forward to check the side mirror, in that last little spot where the window hasn't fogged over, he says, "Not that I'm questioning your motives here, bud, but this is just a smidge dangerous, huh? SALCON commandos out there running around. Remember?"

I ignore him. I'm reasonably confident that we're safe where we are, five miles from the dead bodies of Eric and Dolores Landers, and I hadn't spotted a tail on our exit. "We're good for now," I say. "Tell me something—you know what, forget that, tell me everything, but what I want you to do is start with Dallas. Why'd you kick her out of DPS?"

Satisfied that we weren't followed, and that nobody is slipping up to pierce his neck with a bullet, he shrugs and says, "Because she's nuts. You know that."

The .45 I took off the dead SALCON commando has been waiting patiently in my lap. I slowly turn the barrel around so that it's facing Deke, his left side in particular, then I impatiently tap the grip. "Be specific."

He sees what I'm doing, but he doesn't have anywhere to scoot, so he just looks at me with a mixture of fear, contempt, and mild annoyance. He knows I won't shoot him.

Or will I?

"Put that thing away," he says.

"Be…*specific*."

Deke rolls his eyes. "She wasn't offing her marks like she was supposed to. She was collecting the money but splitting it seventy-thirty with the heroes she was supposed to eliminate. Some took the payoff and disappeared. Others? They've done the, 'You'll believe a hero can die' thing, vanished, probably on an extended vacation with Dallas's thirty percent, and then when the money ran out, they've been resurrecting themselves. I mean, did you know that Billie Bombshell used to be Queen Crush?"

"No shit? I thought she looked familiar."

"Yep. Anyway, it was Lisa that caught on. Sent memos up the chain to get Dallas out, and she didn't handle it too well. She's been terrorizing poor Charlene ever since."

"Damn. At least her compulsive lying thing is legit, huh? I thought for sure she was faking it just to sit around SASS humble-bragging. Hang on a second, though, why's Charlene in that group with her? You'd think…"

Deke pauses long enough with a "cat that ate the canary" look on his face that I have to remind him of the pistol in my hand and its highly effective accuracy at two feet by tapping it again. Beads of sweat roll down his temple where I can see a vein throbbing beneath his aging, thinning skin. "Um…"

"Tell me!" I yell.

He jumps and throws both hands out, pleading. "Charlene's not really an assassin. Never killed a fly. Just some greenhorn DPS agent that we slung into the lion's den without really knowing how far Dallas would take her revenge."

"What? Why?"

"We didn't have a replacement, not until you came along, and it was easier to get Dallas out the door if she had somebody to direct her anger toward. It fit her profile. Give her an outlet, and she'll take the bait."

"Not smart, Deke."

His shrug is so heavy it's almost cartoonish. "I tried to tell 'em. Anyway, Dallas leaked a fake story to Don Donner, and now Charlene has every muscled freak in tights after her. Brave girl. She's made it this long, but we're not sure how much longer we can protect her."

"The hell is she still doing out in public, then? Get her out. Hide her, for God's sake, because between Dallas and every hero gunning for her head, she'll be dead in a month unless you put that girl on an invisible island somewhere in the South Pacific."

Deke pulls a flask from inside his jacket pocket.

He unscrews the lid and takes a long, long swig. When he's finished, he wipes the top and offers it to me.

When in Rome.

It burns going down. Wild Turkey, maybe.

"Seriously, Deke. Get her into hiding."

He says, "I wish it was that easy. We've got her prepped to kill President Palmer in three days."

Eighteen

Two Weeks Earlier, Con't.

This LearJet is big enough to hold my entire tiny ass apartment inside of it, which is why Kimmie sits so far away from me that I'd need a telescope to see the pissed-off frown on her face. After I tossed Daddy Oilbucks halfway across the hangar—and thankfully for him, into a pile of boxed up pillows—it took a little while to calm her down. Him, too, once he shook the cobwebs out. Luckily for me, he was too dazed to get all crazy and rage out on me, but he did throw a couple of wild swings that spun him in circles and sent him back to the ground.

We eventually came to an understanding: after this trip, in which something would be accomplished that would satisfy all involved parties, I was to never, ever, never, ever see his little girl again.

Fine by me. She's got a butt fine enough to chew like bubble gum, but truth be told, Kimmie (or Polly, or Blue Baroness, or White Cloud) is more trouble than she's worth. It's always the hot ones, you know? Crazier than a yard full of escaped mental patients.

Okay, so we're flying, and we're on our way to the Maldives. The inside of this jet is an ugly beige color, but damn if the seats aren't cozy. I'm melting into this thing, and I'd love to take a nap if it weren't for the fact that Kimmie is subconsciously showing every indication that she'll murder me in my sleep. It's a long flight, too. I hope the flight attendant has enough coffee in storage to keep me going.

I take another look at Kimmie. She's got her legs crossed, and her toe is doing that bouncing thing it does when she's annoyed. She's staring out the window with her chin propped up on one hand, hair in a ponytail, ignoring the copy of *Cosmo* in her lap. I wonder what she's thinking about. I can read microexpressions like they're a flashing neon sign, but believe me, deconstructing the mind of a woman is not part of that skill set.

I mentioned how I mentally marry a woman the moment she says hello. It was no different with Kimmie—Polly, then—and she was the same way. About five years ago, we were at this superhero fundraising event in West Palm Beach called *Miles of Muscles* where we walked around a track for a week to raise money for cancer. It was a noble cause, and I was happy to do it, but when I found out that the Monster Masher, the superhero who organized it, had used all those funds to buy a mansion in Miami instead of granting wishes for sick children—let's just say that I didn't hesitate for a second when the FBI called me one evening with a new contract.

Kimmie and I met while we were walking around the track in hundred-degree weather and fifty-thousand percent humidity on the third day. By the end of the event two days later, we had The Preacher marry us on the spot. (Sad side note: he died in an epic battle with Fallen Angel last December. The world mourned. Even the Pope.)

Kimmie and I thought we knew what love was.

Or, maybe our love was true, but she wasn't.

She's not a good person. However, that doesn't mean that I'm not drawn to her like an innocent fly to a bug zapper. I should know better, and I get electrocuted every time.

Still. Look at her. She literally activates the salivation glands in my mouth.

Leo. Get yourself under control.

Do not forget the glee in her eyes when you told her the plan to off Patriotman. I'm not so sure that she wouldn't try to do it for real. Keep an eye on her.

There are times where I wish we could go back and start over, or not even start to begin with. Those first couple of months, I was married to America's

Sweetheart, the lovable, cheery, ass-kicking superhero that everyone loved. *That* was the person I wanted to go to bed with every night. Instead, once she felt comfortable enough to pull back the curtains, I saw that the wizard was really a bitter, self-entitled, petty, jealous, spoiled brat who thought she could get away with whatever she wanted.

That's the thing, see, just like all the other evil good guys that I've eliminated, we have our faults. Some are worse than others. I drink straight out of the milk carton, while Kimmie should be spending ten years behind bars for illegal international trading and a host of other offenses. She's cost the US government billions and they're kindly passing those losses on to you in the form of tax dollars.

She's not so bubbly now, is she?

We may be superhuman, but at our nucleus, we're still *human*.

And that's an imperfect creature.

***

We don't speak through much of the flight, not even when we hit turbulence so bad that I'm wishing one of my powers was flying, like my buddy Superman, and we don't speak in the car on the way to the resort.

She's fuming so viciously that I can feel the heat coming off of her skin. The steam pouring out of her nostrils is like an angry dragon's snout, and I'm positive that she'll spit fire at me before long.

Okay, that's not really true. She's not emitting vaporized water from her nose, but she's pissed.

She ignores me when we check in. She ignores me when we drop our stuff off in the room. She ignores me for the next three hours while we sit on the deck and drink our own individual bottles of mango vodka, waiting on my *doppelganger*, Bart Alonzo, to show up for dinner. We've invited him over to discuss the plan after my "death," and he's dragging his feet down at one of the marinas, waiting to catch a charter out for some kind of fish that are running. I told him to hurry because I sure could use a buffer.

It's not until I follow Kimmie down to the white sands and blue water that she finally decides to grace me with her voice.

"Did you have to throw him?"

"That's what you're pissed about?" I know that's *exactly* why she's mad, but I can't resist poking the badger a little more. This isn't a vacation—it's business—and I spent enough time ruminating over our rocky past to realize that there will be no horizontal muscle flexing underneath the covers, so I figure I don't have much to lose. Anything, really. I add, "I thought you've might've been mad at me for killing off Patriotman. I mean, come on, he's—I'm—a national icon."

"I would kick your spleen into next February if I didn't know you well enough to realize that you're an idiot. He's my dad, Leo. I know you've never gotten along, but don't you dare pull that super shit on him again, you understand me?" She takes her finger out of my chest long enough to slap me on the shoulder, then resumes poking. "He's an eighty-year-old man, and you could've killed him."

I scoff at this and look away. We're in a gorgeous spot—absolutely stunning—like the water is so clear I can see fish swimming on the bottom fifty feet away. The breeze pushes palm fronds around. Small waves lap against the beach. It's hot, but it's paradise, and here we are squabbling about her jerk of a dad.

So what if I tossed his ass? He deserves every— you know what? Never mind. It's not a battle I'm going to win and yeah, maybe it was wrong.

I try not to roll my eyes when I say, "I'm sorry, okay? It was a gut reaction. You saw him. I thought he was coming after me."

She crosses her arms and does that chin waggle thing like she's insinuating, *So? And?*

"He spooked me. I reacted. And besides, he used to run around with The Hulk, didn't he? I thought he had some of the super juice himself."

"Dad's just a meathead, moron. I don't even—oh my God, forget it. How long have we been doing this?"

"Doing what?"

"Having the same arguments. You don't like him, he doesn't like you, and it won't matter after the next couple of days, will it?" She turns away and walks down the beach about five yards before she flops down and begins to dig her toes in the sand. She takes her hairband out and lets her golden hair fall down around her shoulders.

I've hurt her feelings, and I should be ignoring it. Damn it all to hell, now I feel bad.

She puts her forehead on her knees. That makes it worse.

I'm not really seeing her in a new light like this, but it's a shame, you know?

Woulda, coulda, shoulda.

This is how I get into trouble with her. I can see how people get caught up in those abusive relationships and are never able to walk away. Those infamous words, "You don't know what it's like when it's good," keep too many people in chains.

Chains that even superheroes can't break sometimes.

She's right, though. This will be over with in a couple of days, and if I'm going to get away from her and this continuous cycle, I might need to gnaw off my own foot. It has to be done. We can't keep going on like this.

I stroll over to her and sit down, resisting the urge to put my arm around her and at least pretend like I care enough to comfort her. Don't get me wrong, I do. I simply don't want to send any more mixed messages. Come on, I should be out fighting crime, whether it's as Leo Craft the superhero assassin, or as Patriotman, instead of sitting next to my stewing ex-wife who'll likely murder me in my sleep later this evening.

No matter the level of self-importance, or *real* importance to the human race, we've got our problems like everyone else.

I sigh and nudge her shoulder with mine anyway. Some small gesture of regret or care might keep me alive in her presence, and I'm only half-joking about that. "Let's walk over to the yacht. How's that sound? I called ahead a couple of days ago and had them get it prepped for us."

She doesn't answer in the affirmative, but she gets up and heads in that direction. The resort staff has even brought it around for us, and *Misery's Fortune* rocks gently against the small pier.

It's an ancient forty-footer that I picked up years ago when I wanted to "get away from it all," but I love it like a child. We board it and give ourselves a couple of minutes to get our legs adjusted. Kimmie stays silent, pouting, while I check for wear and tear.

Satisfied that everything looks to be in good shape, I encourage her to come up front with me. I roll out a couple of towels, and we sit, side by side.

"So," I say, "what're you going to resurrect yourself as this time? I think all the good colors are taken, you know? I mean, the Mauve Maiden probably doesn't strike fear in the hearts of criminals."

There it is. A smile. An ear-to-ear grin that she struggles hard to keep from turning into a laugh. She's unsuccessful. Kimmie doesn't really laugh. She has this sort of cackle mixed with a honk that sounds like a cross between a blaring car alarm and a donkey with its tail on fire.

Most people find it annoying. Count me as one of them, but damn, it's good to hear it after so long. I'd say it's been years, and for about thirty seconds, this really feels like old times. This almost feels like our honeymoon all over again.

See? It's like I have a stretchy rubber band tied to a

belt loop, and every time I try to run away, it drags me right back.

She's not good for you, Leo. Business only. She's your witness. Accept and move on.

I don't say anything else yet. I let her laughter die out until she's wiping her eyes and cleaning the joyful tears off her sunglasses before I say, "Thanks for coming. You know, for doing this. There aren't many people I could trust with this kind of information." I wait a beat, then add, "I *can* trust you with it, right?"

"Oh, please, Leo. If it means getting Patriotman out of the game—just for spite—and getting my ass back in it, whether it's as the Mauve Maiden or something else, I'm all for it. I'll carry your secret to my grave. And *excuse* me," she says, sounding increasingly annoyed, "but who's kept your 'Leo Craft is Patriotman' secret for the past three years, even after you dicked me over and ruined my career? Who, Leo? Who?"

"You did," I answer, sheepishly. She has a point, and it's not one I'd considered, now that I think about it. In all this time, I've never thanked her for keeping quiet. I "killed" her to keep her safe and as much as she hates me for it, I suppose there's some small measure of gratitude, or the fact that she has feelings for me, that remain underneath her vicious exterior because yeah, she's right, my face isn't plastered all over *Tonight with Don Donner* under some headline reading, "Guess Who?"

"A little thank you would go a long way."

I watch a seagull drift blissfully on the breeze. I envy his freedom. "Thanks, Kimmie. Polly. Whatever. I hadn't thought of it like that. I mean, yeah, I guess I owe you big time, huh?"

She fiddles with a piece of dried seaweed.

There's so much unsaid between us.

"Is it enough that my identity is dying and yours will be resurrected?"

"Probably."

"Probably?"

"Yes."

"Then why do you sound, uh, sad?"

Kimmie tosses the seaweed into the water and brushes off her hands. She pushes her sunglasses higher on her nose and sniffs. It *could've* been a sniffle. Hard to tell. I've never seen her cry before. She says, "It's weird, huh? So many years ago, we were the 'it' couple. God, we looked good, didn't we? You in that red, white, and blue suit, me in those stretchy tights?"

"Your camel toe outfit?"

"Stop," she says, grinning. "I'm being serious. We could've been legends *together*, if you hadn't gotten all righteous and mighty. But here we are, chatting like an old married couple. It feels like the end of something, and it feels so strange to not hate your guts."

"You don't?"

"No, because it'll feel so good to make your idiotic plan a reality."

The knife slides through my ribs before I have a chance to ask her what she means. Only trouble is I don't have to. I'm learning the painful way.

NINETEEN

Present Day

I'm driving Deke's rental car like I stole it.

This isn't my best idea ever, but I'm trying to get to…well, shit, I don't even know where I'm going, honestly. With Deke's revelation that Charlene is the would-be John Wilkes Booth, I had to get on the move because I felt the need to run away from reality.

Deke's in the passenger seat, begging me to slow down, telling me that it wouldn't be smart to get pulled over by the cops. He can pull rank, of course, but will it do any good? All he has to do is flash some creds, and we'll be on our way, right? Normally, that's how it works, but since only a handful of people have ever heard of Direct Protection Services, we might get an escort to the local station while the flatfoot radios ahead to have someone check it out.

I slap the steering wheel and shout, "Damn it!"

"Does that mean you'll slow down?"

"*No…* Yes." I make a left out of the current neighborhood and then at the stop light I turn right, practically on two wheels, onto Highway 50 and cruise toward Falls Church. I spent some time there in what feels like another life, back when Kimmie and I were playing house and living close to the nation's capitol. You know, back when we tried to keep up our 'Real American Couple' persona.

It's too early for the sun to be up, but with all the streetlights, traffic lights, lights from convenience stores, illuminated car dealerships and restaurant parking lots, we might as well be driving through in the middle of the day. I liked it here way back when, but I don't miss it.

I hadn't given Deke a chance to explain himself before I floored it. Now seems like a good time. Besides, if he loses any more circulation in those white knuckles gripping the door handle, I might have to amputate his fingers.

I ease off the gas pedal as I top a little hill, and it couldn't have come any sooner. A police cruiser rolls by going southbound. The patrolman gives me a subtle nod. I see his brake lights flash in the rearview mirror and, thankfully, he decides we're not suspicious enough to tail and call in the license plates. Two reasonably average looking white males driving a rental car—to him, we're probably on our way to the airport or back home after a business meeting. Regardless, he's gone, and I allow myself to unclench.

The brakes squeak when we stop at the next stoplight, and the sound feels like my thought processes—in need of some serious greasing. "Deke?"

He clears his throat. "Time to explain, huh?"

"Here's what we're going to do. You're going to tell me every single fucking detail you can think of. What you know. Who knows what you know. Why Palmer. Why Charlene. Why George Silver. I want it all, Deke, and in exchange—"

"I can't do it, Leo. I don't have the clearance to give you—"

The light turns green and I pull away. I grind my teeth together and try to speak as calmly as possible. "Clearance doesn't matter anymore. You tell me, you walk away, and you disappear forever. Listen to me, man. Think about it. Murdering a president, whether it's an inside job or not, your head is gonna roll. This ain't the '60s, dude. People don't keep their mouths shut; someone will find you just because you took a crap in the wrong bathroom stall. You know this. You *know* it. What're you thinking? *Are* you? *Are* you thinking?"

"Leo, I—"

"Shut up. Just shut up. I like you. I didn't at first but I do now. Past to present. Didn't, do. You tell me everything I need to know, and I'll pay you to walk.

I've got money. More than I'll need, more than you'll
need. I always knew something would happen and that
I'd need to disappear. You don't live the kind of life
I've had and not think about vanishing until you're
ready to meet God Himself. Got it? I'm buying your
answers, Deke, then you're gone. Safe, out, gone. Find
yourself a pretty little lady in a hut somewhere, and sip
sweet drinks out of coconuts. That's my offer."

"And if I say no?"

I jam the barrel of my .45 into his ribs, and I'm not
gentle about it, either. "Then we take a different drive,
one where I know where I'm going, and you won't be
coming back from it. Don't make me do that. Not
when you've got a good twenty years left."

"All right. Jesus. Just get that thing out of my side
before you hit a pothole."

It's a sensible request, and I oblige.

He rolls down his window a couple of inches and
takes a swipe at his forehead. "It's hot in here, ain't it?"

"Deke!"

"All right, all right." He readjusts himself in his
seat and tries to loosen up the lap belt around his beer
belly. "This goes way back, you see, like to the
Watergate days, back when Silver and Palmer were
freshmen senators. Palmer screwed Silver on this
Mideast oil deal—remember all those long lines at the

gas pumps? Hell, I don't even recall what committee it was, but anyway, George Silver has been in it for the long game. Almost forty years have gone by, and he's tried so many different schemes to bring Palmer down, but none of them have worked. None. Not a single one."

"Like what?"

"Paying off sexy interns, bribery, teamster scandals. Everything you can think of. Palmer's too slippery. So, now we're down to one second on the clock, and Silver is trying to throw a Hail Mary."

"By *murdering* Palmer? Seriously?"

"The man holds a grudge. I think he's so fed up and pissed off that none of his shitty schemes have worked: he's finally ready to kill the poor bastard and be done with it. And, he's doing it all under the umbrella of DPS so we can be the ones to run the investigation behind the scenes and clear everybody involved. Sure, the other top agencies will be all over the news, but they're there to tell the media that we have solid leads and we'll eventually arrest Charlene as a patsy. The conspiracy nuts will still be digging through the case files a century from now, but they'll never find the truth."

It occurs to me that I should pull over, detain the guy, and turn him over to the feds, but if I do that,

how am I going to explain my end of the story? I'm
not exactly an innocent snowflake given the contracts
I've accepted. Now that Eric Landers is dead, and
likely the heads of the CIA and FBI, Joe Gaylord and
Conner Carson, I don't have that top layer of
protection. If I go anywhere near a federal building,
claiming to have knowledge of a plot to assassinate the
President, I'm wearing an orange jumpsuit and a black
hood in Guantanamo within twenty-four hours. I
won't have to worry about SALCON—I'll be at the
mercy of good ol' Uncle Sam.

Damn. It looks like I'm in this until I can clear my
name.

Should I bother? Why not disappear now?

I recall that George Silver wanted Patriotman
dead, due to reasons unknown. Does Deke have that
answer? I'm not one to hold grudges for very long. I
react and get shit done before it festers. If I run, if I
hide, he gets away with everything.

"So George Silver is like Lex Luthor and Palmer is
Superman? 'Rats, foiled again'?"

I wonder how my buddy Supes would feel about
me comparing him to Palmer, but he's probably heard
worse.

"Something like that, yeah."

This is big. Real big. But it all seems too easy. "So

what I'm hearing from you is that George Silver has been holding a grudge against Mike Palmer for forty years and the only way to get some piece of mind is to off the dude."

Deke nods. "Yup. It's not that glamorous, but this ain't Hollywood."

"And you and Agent Kelly are willfully following orders? What the fuck, Deke? Are you kidding me? It's murder, man. You're murdering a president."

"Says the guy who kills heroes for a decent paycheck."

"That's different, and you know it. They deserve what they get. Palmer doesn't deserve to die because of some petty, forty-year-old grudge, does he? I've met the guy. He doesn't seem all that bad." As soon as I hear the words come out of my mouth, I know that I've slipped. I was caught up in my mini-tirade and didn't think it through.

"You've *met* him? When? How?"

Oops. No sweat. I can lie my way out of this. You know how nobody has ever figured out that Clark Kent is Superman? In real life, Clark is this bumbling, goofy, *aww-shucks* kind of guy—a nerd, if you will—and only a select group of people know that he slips on the red and blues to become Superman. I know, Lois knows… Steve Rogers. Bruce Wayne. Maybe a couple of others. Anyway, same goes for me. Other than Kimmie, Mom, Phil, Clark Kent, and Bart Alonzo, my double, not a single person knows that I'm Patriotman.

"I, uh, I met him at a fundraiser about ten years ago."

"Oh, gotcha." Deke seems to accept this, with only a hint of suspicion, and I let out a miniscule huff of relief when he doesn't pursue it further.

"I don't... I don't get it. This is—it's insane. How can somebody be that bitter for forty years?"

"If you're surprised by that, then you don't know people very well."

"I thought for sure that it was the VP wanting to get into Palmer's seat. To save face, or whatever, you know? Like get Palmer out of there before his shitty approval rating drags Thomason down with him."

"I'm sure it's crossed the Veep's mind a time or two, but nope."

I flick on my blinker and make a left. I feel too exposed out here on the main highway now that I'm sitting with an accomplice to a Presidential assassination. Just being in the same car with him—and hearing talk of the plans—could put me away for life. "Unbelievable."

"What?"

"That it's so simple."

Deke shrugs and frowns. "Never underestimate the power of…well, the power of being a petty bastard. Some people never grow up."

"Okay, two more questions."

"That's it? Only two?"

"No, I'm just getting started, but let's tackle these two first."

"Let me guess the first one. Why am I telling you?"

"Yes."

He allows the moment to soak in anticipation before he answers in a softer tone. "Second thoughts. It's not right. It hasn't *been* right, Leo, and if anybody can put a stop to this, it's you."

"Thanks for the vote of confidence, but Jesus, man, this is way bigger than me. Second question— why're you and Lisa going through with this? Why help Silver assassinate Palmer?"

"A man will agree to just about anything with a gun to his head, Leo. You know that. I tried to say no. Lisa, too, but you don't get to refuse when a bunch of goons dressed in black show up at your house at three in the morning. Made it seem like an 'offer you can't refuse' thing. Silver himself was standing there beside my bed. Can you believe it? Guy makes house calls to get what he wants. Matter of fact, if this car's bugged or if I've got a micro-device on me somewhere, I got a bullet sandwich waiting for me the minute I'm alone."

"And Agent Kelly? How's she feel about this?"

He pauses, makes a face like it pains him to answer. "She's not on board with me yet. Said I shouldn't tell you, not until we figure out how to save ourselves first, but I've been telling her all along that you can help."

"Jesus."

We're driving through another sleepy, quiet neighborhood, yet the sun is starting to give the eastern sky a warm glow and more dutiful citizens are coming to life. Leaving to beat the traffic, walking their dogs, and squeezing in a quick run before it's off to their cubicles, working for the man. In the meantime, I'm cruising around with a guy who's been coerced, by the Secretary of Defense, into facilitating an assassination of the President of the United States.

Just another Tuesday morning, right?

The general public likes to believe that there are massive conspiracies underfoot when it comes to anything dealing with the government. Like, aliens are real and the government is hiding the truth. Or maybe Lyndon Johnson personally had Lee Harvey Oswald shoot Kennedy from the Texas book depository. Or that 9/11 was an inside job, giving us a reason to invade Iraq for cheaper oil.

The truth is, the simplest explanation is often the correct one. There are no grand conspiracies—I'd *like* there to be, because it would make more sense than the fact that one idiot with a gun can change the course of history. We like to create stories to make up for the fact that a simple act of shitheadedness can alter our lives for the next fifty years. We don't like being out of control on that level. We don't like knowing that our world can be thrown into upheaval by something as simple as a grudge.

When bad things happen on a substantial scale, it's easier to believe that humongous groups of secretive people were driving the school bus to Hell, rather than accept the fact that Fate, or Chance, or one guy with a bad idea can fuck things up for the rest of us.

I ask him, "And you want *me* to fix this? Is that what I'm hearing? You suddenly decide that you've got a conscience, and you're dumping it on me to stop it?"

Deke exhales a long, pitiful, exhausted sigh. "That's about the size of it. I'm too old. Too slow. And I can't die with this on my shoulders. You're a good man, Leo. I know you'll do the right thing. In some ways, you remind me of Patriotman. Could be the way you sorta look like him. Maybe that's why I'm asking you to do some good."

How can you say no to that?

"I'll think about it."

"Good. I appreciate it. It'll mean the world to me if—"

"Hang on, we're not done here yet."

"We're not?"

"Back, like, three weeks ago, when we went to visit Silver at the black site in the mountains?"

"Yeah?"

I explain the entire story to him. What Silver said, why he claimed he wanted Patriotman dead, and that Eric Landers, right before he died, had mentioned that the Secretary of Defense had never liked me— although I didn't say me, as in Leo, because Deke doesn't need to know. Maybe I'll tell him one of these days if any of us make it out of this alive.

"What I want to know, Deke, is why did Silver make up that bullshit story? Why did he *really* want Patriotman dead? You have to know."

Deke's answer confounds me. After all I've seen, done, and heard, I honestly thought I lacked the ability to be truly surprised.

TWENTY

Two Weeks Earlier, Con't.

I heal easily and quickly. That's a benefit of being a manufactured superhuman. You get injected with enough blue goo that's hyped up in a lab, it's easy to feel like nothing can take your life away. I haven't had a needle poked in me in, oh, thirty years, and I've often wondered if this shit will ever just wear off, like batteries dying out.

I'm nearly invincible but injuries still hurt like a son of a bitch, yet they're usually fixed by my internal mechanisms before I step back into a fight. I wouldn't say I'm quite as much of a badass as that Wolverine guy, though I'm pretty close. Here's a quick example: I once fell off a ten-story building after the Dream Demon caught me with a wicked roundhouse kick that I wasn't expecting. I landed, broke my back, and bounced like a basketball. By the time I hit the ground again I was healing and ready to rock.

But this knife in the side of my ribs? It must have pierced a lung, because I can't breathe right. Kimmie pulls away, grinning, and leaves the blade hanging in my side. I'm dizzy. Woozy. I haven't felt this before. Why am I…what's happening…

I manage to utter, "Was that poisoned?" I watch her honk that stupid honk of a laugh as I fall back onto the sand. She leans over and twists the knife, hard, gouging it into my side, tearing flesh and shattering bone.

She says, "Don't worry, I'll still tell your stupid little story about the brozantium. This is just for an extra measure. Makes it look real."

Kimmie may be a fallen hero, but, damn, she does have some muscles in those lithe arms. She's been keeping up with her regimen, maybe for a day exactly like today.

My vision begins to tunnel, the blackness encroaching on the blue water, the blue sky, and the white sands. Waves rock the yacht, and I hear the clang of a metal hook on the mast.

I reach for her. I want to squeeze her throat until it squishes out between my fingers. The darkening circle closes, closes, to a pinpoint of light, and then I'm out.

***

When I wake up, it's pitch black and cool and I'm lying on something hard and metallic. It's cold against my skin. Am I...am I in a morgue drawer? I remember what happened, vaguely. The images in my mind are hazy, gauzy, and I can make out the fact that Kimmie was cackling right before the world went as black as it is now.

Something stretches across my cheeks, and I reach up to feel what's there.

Damn, it's my Patriotman mask. At least they let me keep that on, which is good. Hopefully my true-life identity remained hidden while I was out for...

Shit, what day is it?

And did I survive Kimmie's betrayal, or did she do that on purpose—that whole murdering me thing? Because yeah, I'm not dead.

I shift positions. It's cramped and uncomfortable in here.

A bright, red light emits from somewhere within the drawer, illuminating this enclosed, claustrophobia-inducing coffin. It flashes briefly, giving me time to see that I'm naked from the mask down, and there's a toe tag hanging off my right foot. The red light flashes again, and my ribs ache when I move to discover the source. Whatever she got me with, that crap has a lingering effect.

It flashes a third time, and I have to close my eyes. I already have too many shimmering lights swirling around in my vision.

There it is. I put my hand on a small, plastic box. I trace my fingers around the corners, and it feels like it's about the size of an engagement ring box. On the top is a rounded bulb that might be the LED light that's been flashing. I confirm this by holding my thumb over it and watching the red illuminate under my thumbnail.

It's…what is this thing?

My lungs shut down when I briefly consider the idea that it might be some kind of micro-bomb that Kimmie carried onto the plane. With Daddy Oilbuck's private jet, she wouldn't have to go through security, and this is how I turn into a pile of superhero oatmeal inside a morgue drawer, once and for all.

If that's what this thing is, my only option is escape. As soon as I lift my foot to kick the door open, because certainly some rinky-dink latch can't hold the mighty Patriotman, I hear the thick *kachunk* of the exterior handle. The door swings open, temporarily blinding me with white this time, and I'm rolled out feet first.

Standing above me is a large islander, tanned skin contrasting starkly against the white uniform of a morgue attendant. His hair is the dark color of Deathstrike's uniform, with eyes bluer than Kimmie's outfit back when she was the Blue Baroness. He smiles, showing a sparkling white row of teeth, and pats me on the chest. He smells like coffee and stale cigarettes. "Thank God it worked," he says in stilted English. "They weren't sure that it would."

One wall is taken up with rows of drawers like the one I'd been calling home for some indeterminate amount of time. The metal wall is full of them, and it's so clean I can almost see my reflection. A row of three fluorescent lights hang overhead, their brightness clawing into my retinas. I see a bay of windows to my left, and beyond that, there's a cluttered desk with a small lamp, and what looks to be a five-inch television screen playing a rugby match.

So, a hospital? How'd I get here?

"What's that?" I say, sitting up. "Thank God what worked?" I'm beyond being modest, but I ask the dude for a robe, or my clothes, or something, to cover up the fact that my junk is splayed out on this sliding drawer like a snake basking in the sun.

"Oh, right." He spins around, looking for something, and slips a white sheet off a dead body at my twelve o'clock. "Here."

I cringe and feel guilty, but the old woman on that

morgue table is most definitely a goner, and she's probably well past modesty, too. I'm probably imagining the scent of embalming fluid as I wrap the blanket around me. I hold up the black box with the red light that's still flashing. "Is this some kind of…what is this thing?"

"They said it was a miniature seismograph that would send a signal when you started moving again. Didn't know for sure if it would get past all that metal. Here you are, though, Mr. Patriot, alive and kicking. Hey, you want some coffee?"

"No." I shake my head. I change my mind. "Yes. How long have I been in there?"

Sam, according to his nametag, checks his watch, then matches it against the clock on the wall. "Thirty two hours and change."

"Feels longer." He hands me a cup of coffee that smells like motor oil and tastes like *stale* motor oil. "Sam?"

"Yessir?" He looks overeager to please and thoroughly excited that I used his name. He's a gentle giant. Might make a good replacement for the Beast Machine if anybody ever wanted to resurrect that identity again.

"What would've happened if the signal didn't get out?"

"Then I wait another twenty four hours and pull you out myself."

"Dead or alive?"

"They said you'd be alive."

"They? You keep saying 'they.'"

"A lady and a guy."

"They have names?"

Sam shakes his head, begins rummaging through some boxes on a shelf nearby. "Now where'd I put your stuff?" he says, muttering to himself.

"Blonde lady and a guy about my size? Maybe he looked like me quite a bit."

Sam shrugs. He's uncomfortable, hiding something, or a little of both.

"Sam?"

"Here they are," he says, pulling my shorts and a bloody t-shirt out of a box marked "S.P." He also pulls out my Patriotman uniform and holds it up. "You want to put this back on? Or the normal clothes? Normal clothes might be good, only your shirt here, it's not in such good shape."

He's smiling, holding my things out to me, trying to get me to gloss over who delivered me. I repeat myself. "Focus, Sam. Blonde lady and a guy that might've looked like me?"

"Well, um, the medics and police brought you in,

dressed in your uniform, then they had her and the guy identify you. But—uh—yeah, she's blonde. Real pretty, too. About this tall," he says, holding his hand up indicative of Kimmie's height.

"That's her. No name?"

"No, she wouldn't say."

"The cops, they're out looking for my murderer?"

"It's all over the news. Nobody knows nothing, but that lady, she says she saw some guy attacking you."

"What about the man with her? Where'd he go?" While Sam thinks about his answer, I take my shorts from him and find my ratty flip-flops in the bottom of the container. I rummage around in some of the other boxes nearby and find a blue t-shirt with a seagull on it that's a bit too tight, but it'll have to do. "Look," I say, urging him on, "I know you looked under the mask, that's why you're futzing around like this."

"You know that?" His eyes go wide in disbelief. "Are you psychic? Is that one of your superpowers?"

I have to laugh. I can't help it. He seems embarrassed, so I reassure him that it's fine. This situation is too far gone to care about one more person knowing my identity.

"Oh," he says, seemingly disappointed. "That would be cool too, huh? My dad says you can absorb the powers of others. That's how come you're so awesome."

This makes me think of my dad. Or step-dad, really. Phil. I need to go pay him a visit when I get back to the States. He's a good guy, even if he has gotten a little curmudgeonly lately.

"I wish, bud. That'd make this job a lot easier. Okay," I say, finally dressed, "I've got three questions for you and all I want is clear answers. Can you do that for me? Can you do that for Patriotman?"

He lifts an eyebrow at me, slightly confused. "Are those two of the three questions?"

I chuckle. Sheesh. I'd be in some seriously pissed off, rage-induced, total blowup mood if it weren't for this big honking dude unintentionally providing comic relief. "No, Sam. Here's the first one. I know you peeked under the mask because you got that sheepish look written all over your face. Did the guy that was in here with the pretty lady look anything like me, and if he did, did he leave behind any messages?"

Sam is suddenly really interested in the tops of his shoes, but he answers anyway, like a little kid admitting he stole a cookie from the jar. "Yes, sir. Exactly like you. Like a twin or something. He said to tell you when you woke up, if you ever needed him again, he'd be at the spot with the thing. Said you'd know what that meant."

I do. It means Bart Alonzo went back home to Barcelona, to his magnificently overdone house that I've mostly paid for all these years, where *the thing* is this giant statue of a nude Marilyn Monroe, only the sculptor screwed it up royally, so now it more or less looks like The Thing from the Fantastic Four.

Either the police let him go, or Bart Alonzo disobeyed orders and skipped out.

"Good, good." I look up and around the room, checking the corners, not discovering what I'm searching for. I see no surveillance cameras, and, I figure if there were any, Sam wouldn't have pulled me out and allowed a dead man to walk around the room.

I reach up and pull off my mask. It's sort of freeing, in a way, to stand here in front of an average citizen, intentionally revealing my identity. The weird thing is, I feel more naked than when I didn't have a stitch of clothing on. Sam gasps, and I shrug like it's no big deal. "Question two, buddy. What about the pretty lady…she say anything?"

He reaches into the pocket over his left pectoral muscle, which is literally about the size of a small ham. I'm not kidding. This guy would make a great Beast Machine. He pulls out a small note and hands it to me.

"She said to give you this."

I unfold the note and read it out loud because I'm sure he's already snooped on it, too. "Dear Dumbass, your plan was stupid, mine was much better, and this way, at least it looked real. The cops and the media think you're dead. Don't ever call me again. See you on the other side. Never yours, Kimmie. P.S. I hope the knife hurt like hell." I clear my throat and raise an eyebrow. "Can you believe we were in love once?"

Sam squints at me. "Is that the third question, sir?"

I take a deep breath, shake my head, and grin. "No, Sam. No, it's not. Third question is, where's the closest place to get a burger? I'm starving."

I invite Sam to come along with me, because he knows too damn much, and I'll need to debrief him. Plus, he's huge, and right about now I could really use an ally.

"You mean that?" he asks, surprised. "I can come with you?"

"Surprise question, Sam… If I asked you to drop everything and become the new Beast Machine, my supreme ally, are you able to walk away and do it?"

The size of his smile is big enough to disrupt gravity. "Let me get my keys."

TWENTY-ONE

Present Day

Twenty-five years ago, I was a young, fledgling superhero who'd only just come to battle the ins and outs of navigating life as a high school teenager. My identity as Patriotman was a secret, of course, and has remained that way since, but back then, I'd barely figured out how to french kiss a girl before I started fighting supervillains on a worldwide stage. Mom and Phil were conscientious objectors, but how do you put chains on a typical teenager, let alone one with the strength, speed, and agility of a hundred Olympians combined?

More or less, the only thing I couldn't do was fly. I didn't mind that so much because I figured Clark had the market cornered on being the guy flying around in blue tights and a red cape. Besides, I'm a manufactured superhuman, not otherworldly.

My first car was a Dodge Dart. My first girlfriend was a young lady named Amanda who had a heart-melting smile and enjoyed making out with the entire football team after we went to our junior prom. My first F was in History. My first cassette tape, purchased with my own money earned from mowing lawns, was *Licensed to Ill* by the Beastie Boys.

My first major confrontation with a supervillain— which managed to get aired on national television— was against a guy who went by the name of Suckerpunch. He wasn't necessarily one of the physical-type supervillains, but more of an intellectual, unparalleled genius. He had managed to stage a bevy of bank robberies so massive that it had the entire city of New York on a lockdown unlike any they'd ever seen. Every available cop, authority figure, or professional suit with a gun scoured the city searching for this guy and his band of cronies. Looking back on it, the execution was nearly flawless. Twelve banks in twelve minutes scattered far enough apart that the police couldn't figure out which block of the city to tackle first.

That day, Suckerpunch had put The Joker to shame in terms of cunning corruption and sheer brilliance of implementation.

I caught up with him in the middle of Central Park.

He was tall, dressed in a black pinstriped suit, and wore a mask that resembled a Doberman Pinscher.

We fought. Hard.

I was young and inexperienced. I charged ahead like a bull and with the strength of one. He outwitted me at every turn. I landed a few punches here and there, but I was severely outmatched when it came to the intellectual aspect of fighting a good fight.

Or in his case, a sneaky, dirty, dastardly, underhanded one, but as they say, work smarter, not harder.

He won, and escaped, leaving me battered, bruised, and bloody, yet the good news was, I had distracted him long enough to allow the police to capture his crew and their truckloads of money. The only thing he got away with was the couple million in cash that he carried in a ratty briefcase. I probably shouldn't mention that he beat me one-handed, because he held onto that damn thing the entire time, often using it as a weapon.

I got my ass handed to me. It is what it is. On the national news, no less, but in the twenty-five years since then, I haven't lost a single battle, and I feel like I can personally thank Suckerpunch for teaching me what I needed to learn that day. The only problem is, the dastardly bastard disappeared and never committed another crime.

That we know of, at least.

George Silver, the handsome, debonair, eloquent

senator from the great state of Virginia personally extended his hand in gratitude. He'd been in New York that day for a fundraising event and was so overcome with pride for a young superhero that was so gracious in defeat, he invited me onto *Tonight with Don Donner* and put my face in front of the world. *Kapow*, instant notoriety.

All of this comes flooding back to me as soon as I hear Deke say, "Did you ever wonder why they call George Silver 'The Doberman'? Most people think it's because he's so vicious, you know? When he's got an idea about something, he latches on with a full set of fangs and won't let go until you give the right command. As far as I know, he's the one that came up with the nickname for himself."

I feel lightheaded. My legs go numb, as do my feet and hands. The ever-present smell of Deke's overpowering aftershave becomes too much to bear, and I have to roll down my window. The breeze feels cool and refreshing on my face but it barely soothes my sense of…I guess it's remorse. Shock? Regret? I manage to squeak out, "Go on," as the bile climbs up the back of my throat.

"Get this," Deke says. "I don't ever go into things blindly—call it a byproduct of being in this field for too long—so when I was first invited into DPS, I dug up some dirt on everyone I could find, everybody involved. Lisa, the director of DPS, Crenshaw and Hawthorne, you name it, because you never know when you're going to need a safety net. You've heard that 'leap and the net will appear' bullshit? No, sir. Give me soft landing already there waiting."

We've been driving in circles long enough for the traffic to start piling on. I'm exhausted, so I pull into a parking lot and zip through one of those coffee kiosks for a quick pick-me-up. Deke stops talking about the shit he knows regarding Lisa Kelly long enough to order a dry cappuccino, and then we're moving again once the steaming to-go cups get handed over. I find a spot to park under a maple tree at the corner of the lot. I back in because you can't be too careful about a quick getaway.

Deke sips his cappuccino then wipes the foam off his upper lip.

"You were saying?"

"Right. Yeah. Pretty much the entire DPS crew is fairly clean. Lisa worked at a Hooters back when she was at NC State, but other than that, they're all normal, right?"

"Except for...what? Because otherwise, you wouldn't be telling me this shit if there wasn't an exception."

"That's just it, see. It took me quite a while to unearth the fact that Silver was the brainchild behind DPS, so I didn't start looking into his history until about six months after I was running all over the damn country cleaning up messes."

"Why would it matter who set it up?"

"You can't be that naïve, Leo. Really? It matters who pulls the strings, because it matters who's got control of the money. Money talks—"

"And your bullshit is starting to smell. Get on with it." I've already figured out what he's going to tell me, but I want to hear it from his lips.

He rolls his eyes and takes another sip. "I traced George Silver's history all the way back to the day he first started campaigning for office as some smalltime lawyer in Richmond, Virginia. I went through campaign contributions, public appearances, earmarks, everything I could find. From today, counting back twenty-five years, he's as clean as surgeon's hands. But, from August 23rd, 1986, back to July 4th, 1970, there are numerous reports of missing funds, interns filing reports that seem like they were totally swept under the table, all sorts of stuff that should have landed a normal Joe in prison. And I'm assuming you remember what happened on August 23rd, 1986?"

I hate being reminded of that day. "Patriotman got

his ass handed to him by Suckerpunch, then George Silver invited him on Don Donner's show and called him a national hero. Everybody knows that, so I'm assuming you're going to tell me why I should care."

He holds up his index finger and grins. "One report."

"And?"

"Totally buried in a file box and shoved on some back shelf. Had to visit the precinct that took the eyewitness reports of Patriot's battle with Suckerpunch."

"Why would that matter?"

"On the day those guys fought, Silver was in the city for a fundraising event, right? Only problem is, he didn't show up. The lady that organized it, she remembers he called ahead and told them he couldn't make it. Bad egg salad or some shit. Anyway, he shows up that night on *Don Donner*, with Patriotman, looking as sparkly and fresh as ever. I watched it that night, so I didn't know about him cancelling, but I specifically recall how wide-eyed he was to be standing beside the next big thing in superhero names, you know? I realize it was a huge leap, but something—intuition, I guess—made me go watch the video replay of that episode, and the portion of the battle that was televised. It didn't seem like anyone ever caught on to the fact that he had knowledge of some of the battle elements *before* the cameras got to Central Park."

I almost choke on my coffee. "No shit? How'd you know that?"

He points at his chest. "I was there. I was a beat cop back then, and I watched the entire battle from a distance. No way am I getting in the middle of that, not for thirty thousand a year and a small pension. Long story short, I'm reading through the files of the reports from that day, and there's one eyewitness testimony from a little old lady, like, eight hundred years old, who saw a man running away from Central Park. She swore on her life that the guy ran by her and he was taking off a Doberman mask, like Suckerpunch used to wear, and he looked exactly, in her words, "like that handsome man in the newspaper today, that Silver fellow from Virginia."

"And nobody followed up on that?"

"The officer's notes questioned her credibility, and by that I think he meant her sanity, and that was it. And now you know."

"George Silver was Suckerpunch."

"You scared him straight, Leo."

This time, I really do choke on my coffee. "Me?"

Deke winks. "I'm good at keeping secrets, especially when I need help."

Ah, the blue sky peeks out from behind the clouds of misinformation and all this cloak and dagger nonsense. "So you're bribing me to make this thing with Silver and Palmer go away?"

"Something like that, but you're close. I'd even go as far as saying you're a smart cookie."

"And you're a real bastard."

He holds up his to-go cup. "Cheers!"

"My God, how long have you known? Does anyone else?"

"Couple weeks. Not a soul knows, not even Lisa, and she's like a daughter to me. And, let me think...oh, I pieced it together when you came back from the Maldives and had no body to show for it. I can't place why—maybe it's that intuition thing again—but I had a feeling about you from the first day we met in the airport. You looked...familiar in a déjà vu way. Something like that.

"When you came back from the Maldives, and it was all over the news, like that same day, and it seemed to me like it was too quick, like it should've taken longer to hit the wire. Almost like—almost like you did the deed, then called it in to the media yourself and used that lady to tell the story, and I'm thinking, why would he do that? Why not give himself a chance to at least get out of the country before the locals are all over it? I put it together when you wouldn't tell us where the body was. I've looked at every single one of your case files, Leo. You don't operate that way. You're proud of what you do. Same way a cat brings a dead bird home and lays it on the doorstep like an offering. I put it together then. *Vibes.* I get vibes."

I'd put my .45 away, but now seems like just as good a time as any to shove it in his ribs again. He jumps when I do, and I wait on his face to ease out of its contorted fear before I ask, "And are those same vibes telling you that I could easily put a bullet in your gut and take away your trump card?"

He holds up a shaky hand. "Don't pull the trigger, okay? Let me show you something." He reaches for the lapel of his suit jacket, and at that moment, I know exactly what he's going to show me.

The only thing that matters now is who's on the other end of that wire.

TWENTY-TWO

Present Day, Again, and Staying There

Since Sam came back with me from the Maldives, he's been staying in an apartment I keep here in the northern Virginia area. While I'm on-call as Patriotman, I often have to make appearances at the White House to accept awards and shake hands, doing an overly exorbitant amount of glad-handing with sleazy Hill types that make me wish I could carry a small bottle of sanitizer somewhere in my uniform.

But, since I've been in mini-retirement for the past three years while I attempt to cleanse the world of shitty good guys, I've pretty much been paying rent on a place I see only when I'm brought to the East Coast to purge a mark in the area. So, it's good that Sam has been there for a couple of weeks now. Maybe he cleaned the mold off the shower.

Deke and I are sitting here in this parking lot only a mile away from my second home, where Sam is probably just waking up. He's been here training, day after day, lifting, learning, and enjoying his time as he readies himself to become the new Beast Machine, complete with upgraded battle armor and weapons, all courtesy of my bank account.

I don't mind. Patriotman has been in need of a good sidekick for well over a decade, and, with Sam's size, he's a perfect replacement. Once we got back from the Maldives, we got in touch with Hank Cagle, the original Beast Machine, and got his full blessing. Hank is generously donating his time to help train Sam, and he even contributed his favorite helmet to the cause, telling us he was proud to see the ol' boy getting some action again.

With Deke in the car, I'd been slowly making my way in this direction for the simple fact that—while I may like him—I rarely trust a government agent. They're good for passing along information, and for unintentionally putting wrenches in your gears, and that's about it. Otherwise, they're big proponents of the CYA Method—Cover Your Ass.

I had a hunch something was up with Deke, especially considering the fact that he was following me from the Pacific Northwest and showed up in Eric Landers's neighborhood.

If all they wanted to do was tail me, then why not call in an area-based DPS agent and have him riding my bumper from a distance? I know Deke was assigned to me, specifically, but from what I know of him, he's not the type of guy to go out of his way when there's a shorter distance from point A to point B.

Something is afoot, and that's been confirmed, but I have no idea what.

Deke sits there in the passenger seat with a smug grin that I want to smack off his stupid, fat face. Dickhead. He thinks he's got me, and maybe he does, but about the only thing he can do is out my true identity to a reporter.

So what if every one of my superhero buddies turns on me for eliminating our own kind? I have the power and the strength to fight back. It might be a bitch of a few months, but eventually they'll calm down once they see that I've been in the right, for doing what I'm doing, all along.

It might be tough going up against Clark if he chooses to come after me, but that would be like two brothers fighting for different sides in the Civil War. A Confederate and a Union soldier meet on the battlefield, stare each other down, and walk away to fight a different fight.

I hope.

Well, now that I think about it, there's only one thing that would make me shit my pants. I need to figure out whether or not I should be glad I'm wearing dark brown slacks.

Meanwhile, if I could get Sam down here…

To distract Deke, I scream, "Turn it off," shove the barrel of my .45 against his forehead, and then quickly jam my left hand in my pocket to grab my cell phone.

Shit. I can't text in my pocket without looking. I'm not a twelve-year-old girl.

Forget it. I'm going for it. No time to waste considering the people on the other end of that wire already know that Leo Craft is Patriotman.

I press the barrel harder against Deke's forehead and yank my cell phone out. A couple of taps later and I hear the slow ringing in my ear.

Deke tries to pull further away from the barrel and says, "I wouldn't compromise whoever that is. It wouldn't be smart, bud."

"Shut up."

"I'm just saying—"

I hear a groggy, "*Yeah, uh… 'lo?*" from Sam on the other line.

"Tell Mom I'll be home late for dinner," I say, then hang up. That's code for, "I'm in trouble, and use the cell's GPS to come find me." I'm going to use Deke's trick to find me to have help find *us*. Sam and I have worked on a number of these options, like, "Put the cat out, would you?" means, "I'm going into battle, clear my internet history if I don't make it back." I trust that he's been able to master all the technological devices I dumped in his lap when we were back on the mainland. I remember telling him, "You'll need to figure these out," to which he'd replied, "Can't I just beat people up with you?"

Come on, come on, come on. Find me, Sam.

Deke tries to shake his head, squinting at me, confused, but it's hard for him to move his neck because I'm absolutely trying to push the barrel through his skull. I reach into his jacket and pull out the wire and the device it's attached to. Some fancy contraption that I've never seen before—a metallic gray box about the size of an iPhone with a small, digital screen counting up the minutes of recording time. This thing has been going for a couple of hours.

I calculate that back to the moment Deke approached me outside of Landers's house. Briefly, I think that maybe it's nothing more than a digital voice recorder, a decoy, and this will be a simple fix, but those hopes melt when I see *LTE* in the upper left corner. It's broadcasting, and goddamn it, they've heard every word.

I throw it to the floor and smash it with my heel. "*Who*, Deke?"

He doesn't answer. He flashes a look over my

shoulder, like he's waiting on someone too. Or, could be he's trying to pull an old trick; 'Ha, made you look!' in an attempt to distract me. I vote for the latter and keep my eyes on him.

Bad move.

It seems like they come out of the sky, materializing everywhere.

Black commando suits. Weapons ready. They're quiet. They don't need to shout. They know they've got me surrounded. Only thing is I have a gun to Deke's head, but maybe they don't care about that so much, given who it is.

And yeah, I'm glad I'm wearing brown pants, because the worst possible scenario just came true.

SALCON commandos swarm on the car, laser sights, thirty of them at least, pointing at the center of my chest.

I back off of Deke and hold my hands in the air. The .45 dangles from my thumb.

Deke reaches over and takes it from me, smiling.

There's an indentation in his forehead where the barrel buried itself in his skin.

One of these days, I'm going to use that fucking thing as a bulls-eye.

***

In total, there are about forty-five armed SALCON commandos surrounding me as I'm yanked from the driver's side of the car. Ordinarily, forty-five armed men wouldn't be too much of a problem, particularly if they're low-grade schmucks that somebody like Sergeant Evil hired for five bucks an hour to guard his—*ahem*—"impenetrable" palace. I've fought more at once, truth be told, but you don't want to mess around with these guys. Next to the elite Special Forces of the United States military, like SEALs and Green Berets, these guys are probably third in line for the most badass group of soldiers on the planet.

I relent to their pulling and dragging because while I may be nearly invincible, and begin healing on wounding contact, my body is definitely not equipped to handle the exploding shells fired from a SALCON 24T automatic rifle, made by Smith & Wesson.

One of them, a big guy about Sam's size, says to another one, "Standard cuffs? Are you kidding me? He'll snap those things like they're made out of taffy, private. Get the goddamn electro-bar out." The stitching over the right side of his chest says his name is Gordon. A standard issue military mustache that looks like a sleeping caterpillar covers his upper lip. Maybe I could punch him, on principle.

Not a good idea, Leo.

Seconds later, a skittish, totally freaked out kid of about twenty-five years old approaches me with nostrils flaring and his fight-or-flight juice kicked into high gear. He's Lewis, apparently. "I'm sorry, Mr. Patriot, sir. If you'd just let me…"

Gordon barks, "Don't play patty cake, soldier. Get it done."

I hold out my balled fists, wrists up, and let him attach the electro-bar—first the right, then the left. I can feel the barely detectable thrum of electricity running through these things. It makes my skin tingle, and I know that if I struggle too much, it'll deliver enough voltage to stop an elephant's heart.

Gordon grabs me by the neck, guides me to the back of a nearby van and shoves me inside. Twelve SALCON commandos follow. For an extra measure of security, Lewis—who was volunteered again—shakily attaches a chain from the electro-bar to the floorboard. Like I'm going anywhere.

Right now, I'm letting it happen. I'll wait for the proper opening. I'll also wait for the appropriate opportunity to shove my foot so far up Deke's ass, he'll look like a corndog.

The rear doors slam shut and we're encased in shadows, the only light coming from the two small windows at the back of the van. The driver wastes no time in getting up to speed as he hurtles us out of the parking lot. He squeals a right turn and heads northbound.

I spot Sam running down the sidewalk, armor flailing loosely because he doesn't know how to attach it properly yet, or he was in too much of a hurry. I'm betting on the former. He's got a long ways to go before he's truly fit to become Beast Machine. I have to give the poor guy credit though, he's moving ten times faster than I thought he'd be able to by now. It doesn't matter, however, because Hank Cagle wouldn't be able to catch us at this speed either.

Sam pulls up, limping, grabbing his hamstring. He thrashes his arms and curses at the sky.

Too little, too late, Sam. Not that it would've done any good.

In all the commotion, yelling, guns waving, and jostling, they shoved me in here without thinking to check my pockets. The only hope I have left is that Sam will keep his wits enough to continue tracking the GPS positioning of my cell phone.

God only knows where they're taking me, and I can only think of one reason why.

My best guess is, I'm a dead man.

SALCON is super-pissed that I've been

eliminating some of its most important and well-regarded members over the last three years. The NSA, CIA, FBI, or any of the other international government agencies I've worked for haven't been too choosy or cautious when it came to selecting marks for elimination.

There's a credo among the assassins I know, especially the ones in SASS. You only take out the ones who really deserve it, and even then, it's a hard thing to do because millions of faithful fans around the world have to mourn the death of someone they looked up to.

If they only knew.

This goes doubly true for me, considering I'm fighting for both sides.

I've never eliminated someone simply because some D.C. string-puller had a hard-on for watching an old enemy blink out of existence.

In the eyes of SALCON, none of this matters. I've been offing superheroes and upsetting the world balance while they've worked so hard to maintain peace and ensure that people of my kind can live a life of equality. Whether they've chosen to do it on purpose or not, they've continually turned a blind eye to the fact that there are horrible people wearing the white hats of the good guys.

They found out Eric Landers was calling the shots, and likely Joe Gaylord and Conner Carson, too. Ronald Kidman in Australia is probably a goner, as is Theodore Carlisle of England, Phan Thanh Chu of Vietnam, and Elizabeth Canterbury of our polite neighbors from up north.

If they do that, if they go through with knocking off all those important people…

That's all out war.

Supers versus citizens.

No, they wouldn't. It doesn't make sense for them. Not financially. Not politically.

Then what in the hell are they up to?

The soldier beside me, Miller, I take it, slides the infamous, black SALCON hood over my head. Phil warned me about this.

I probably should've listened to him a long time ago.

TWENTY-THREE

Present Day

We bumble and rattle along in the van for what feels like days. It's probably closer to an hour; it seems that long because these guys are stone-cold statues. I mean *quiet*—like I can't even hear the one next to me breathing.

I have no clue where we could be going, and it's a given that none of these goobers will give me a clear answer, or open their mouths at all, so what I do is, I think, because I'm good at that when I'm stuck. I try to process everything that's happened to me over the past month.

First, Agent Lisa Kelly and Agent Deke Carter of Direct Protection Services—agents belonging to a clandestine organization so underground that the President doesn't know about it—approach me in the Portland airport with serious knowledge of my activities as a superhero assassin. That one's easy: interdepartmental sharing.

Or something.

They tell me that there's a plot to assassinate

President Palmer and that they have reason to believe that it's a member of a superhero assassin support group known as SASS. I decide it's a dumb name, accept the assignment and join the group anyway, because no matter how much of a screw-up President Palmer is, he's a nice guy and probably doesn't deserve to die. Well, except for the fact that he initiated these murderous operations against filthy superheroes, which I gladly joined, because I got sick and tired of the assholes out there doing horrible crap under the guise of good.

I went to a couple of the meetings, met some interesting people, then Agents Kelly and Carter showed up at my place asking me to knock off Patriotman. I questioned it, they took me to see…George Silver, which supposedly surprised even them. At this point, I'm thinking Deke knew all along.

Silver gives me a bullshit story about Patriotman turning his back on the American people and his original would-be assassin has a bit of Stockholm Syndrome or got brainwashed, whatever, and is intending to murder the president at Patriotman's behest.

As if it wasn't weird enough already…

I decided to eliminate my alternate identity as Patriotman—because I can always resurrect under a new identity—just to play along with Silver's scheme and try to figure out what in the hell he's up to.

Kimmie did me the favor of making it look real. Point goes to her, I guess, because I never saw that coming.

Okay, what else?

The van bounces, rattles, and I finally I hear the guard next to me groan.

We keep moving. It feels like we're off road. I imagine we're heading to some SALCON stronghold in the middle of nowhere.

I'm not looking forward to this meeting or whatever it is. I imagine they have plans to line me up in front of a firing squad.

Get back to the past, Leo. Look for answers to save your ass.

So then, I went to yet another SASS meeting because I was under the assumption that the murder of President Palmer was still going to be perpetrated by someone in that group. I'd visited a bunch of the members and gotten no vibes, but then, Charlene asked me how I could sit there and allow Dallas to take credit for *my* work.

I learned how she knew *that* when Deke told me that Charlene is actually an employee of DPS.

All of that freaked me out, so I went to see Eric Landers, who was murdered.

I met Deke outside of the house, who told me that Phil was dead, possibly at the hands of Charlene, possibly at the hands of Dallas.

Oh God, Phil. For a couple of brief hours, I'd glossed over the fact that my dad was dead.

Phil...Dad... You were right. I should've listened. I should've kept my mouth shut and fought the bad guys like a hero is expected to do. I feel awful, you know, because I've been lying to you and everybody else all along. Doing this, killing the bad good guys, it was never about the money. I always said that because it was easier than trying to explain that good people can also carry evil in their hearts. What I did may have been hypocritical, but I feel like it was the right thing to do. Murder or thinning out the number of evil people in a different way...maybe you can't justify it. Maybe you can't. *The only thing I do know is, having people believe I was motivated by greed, like Kimmie, was a helluva lot easier than explaining that I was trying to right a wrong in a bad way, for the greater good. So, yeah. I'm sorry. You're gone now, and I'm about to be. Was it worth it?*

The jury is still out, but for now I'm gonna say hell yes.

We bounce on another pothole so hard, it jostles my electro-bar, sending a jolt of electricity through my arms, down through my chest, and into my abdomen.

My heart flutters hard for a moment, but it actually does some good, snapping me back to the present.

Where was I?

George Silver wanted me—or, Patriotman—dead because he's an asshole, and he used to be Suckerpunch, a.k.a The Doberman. According to Deke, he's also the one behind the plot to assassinate Palmer for a forty-year-old grudge.

Deke, evidently, is a two-faced bastard, who's also working with, or for, SALCON.

Should I believe anything he said?

I don't know.

I'm so thoroughly confused that I barely know which questions to ask, and they may not be the right ones at all.

Why would DPS bother sending Charlene into the SASS meetings if they planned to have her assassinate Palmer and be the patsy all along?

How did SALCON find out everything that they know? Did Deke tell them?

Why get me involved? Okay, that one might be easy. If Deke was lying about only discovering my identity recently, then he could've told Silver that I was Patriotman, Silver plays like he doesn't know how to get me to kill off my identity, and then the man behind the mask…

The man behind the mask becomes the patsy for everything.

Oh my God. Silver must be working for SALCON, too.

They're going to have Charlene kill President Palmer and blame me, then the subsequent investigation by the DPS will reveal that Leo Craft, some crazy nobody, was murdering superheroes and also assassinated the President of the United States of America.

Silver knocks off two personal grudges that he's harbored for decades, SALCON gets their revenge on me for offing their constituency and has a name to publicly announce and...

What am I missing?

Where does that leave the other members of SASS?

A cold chill runs down my spine. I have a feeling I might have something to do with that as well.

TWENTY-FOUR

Present Day

The van skitters to an abrupt halt on gravel. That sound is unmistakable.

I hear both of the rear doors open and then the voice of Gordon, the SALCON commando in charge. "Get that pile of cow dung outta here," he says. "Watch him, though."

They don't remove my black hood, but I can hear the sound of the chain jangling as someone unhooks the electro-bar from the floorboard. Next, I'm being dragged to my feet and marched to the rear of the van. "Step down, shitbird," says Gordon.

I decide at this point, a little shock is worth the reward, so I process the general area where his voice came from. I whip my foot out in a hard forward kick and feel the toe of my boot connect underneath his chinstrap. Immediately, a harsh blast of voltage wrenches my body into an awkward contortion, but it's slightly satisfying to hear Gordon hit the ground, spitting and cursing.

The two commandos holding me get a dose of the

shock, too, since they had their hands wrapped around my arms, and I can feel them shaking on the floor of the van beside me. Maybe they're dead. Who knows? Who cares?

Gordon groans again, and a string of curse words *ratta-tat-tat* out of his mouth.

The shock of the electro-bar passes, and I feel more sets of hands on me, dragging me out of the van. I'm guessing it's Gordon getting his revenge, because the next thing I know, there are repeated shots from a rifle butt jamming into my stomach.

He has to realize that it's not doing any good, right? I've taken a horn to the gut from the Purple Rhino that felt like a feather's tickle.

Ah, well, let him have his fun. If I keep him agitated, maybe it'll keep him off guard, giving me an advantage.

When the barrage stops, I cough and whimper as if it had done some damage and then act like it's painful to straighten myself up. I groan and say, "Is that all you got?"

Pop!

Rifle butt, right to the nose. Okay, that one actually hurt a little bit, and my eyes begin to water. Superhuman or not, a good shot to the old honker can be effective. Could be that Gordon has studied the strengths and weaknesses of each of some of the superhero heavies, in case a situation like this ever arose.

He laughs as the multiple sets of hands squeeze tighter around my arms. "All right, shitbird. How'd that one feel?"

"Your sister hits harder."

Pop!

Ouch. Damn it.

Pop!

Son of a—

Pop!

"Enough!" bellows a voice to my left. That, too, is unmistakable. I've only heard the guy on television. Never met him in person, nor had any desire to, but if I were blind, truly blind, I could pick that voice out of a thousand screaming fans at a rock concert. It's high-pitched and rough, like someone took steel wool to harp strings.

It's The Minion, which is ironic, since he's actually the Supreme Leader of SALCON.

And it's funny because he was second in command to Mischief, who used to be the leader. Rumors have swirled for roughly a decade that The Minion knocked off Mischief to take over his spot.

Do I give a crap who is running the damn thing?

Nope.

My eyes are watering so badly that when the black hood is snatched off my head, I can barely make out the black shapes of the skittish commandos. I blink, hard, trying to squeeze the water clean, like a set of windshield wipers, and believe it or not, I taste a drop of blood on my upper lip. Damn. The dickwad actually bloodied my nose.

That hasn't happened since, what, 2005 when I fought Eradicator in Kansas City?

I'll have to give Gordon credit. He's stronger than I expected.

By size and shape, I can make him out in the blur. He's standing at my twelve o'clock, along with the entire horde of SALCON commandos. Deke Carter, the only one in the crowd not wearing black, is at my eleven, and off the left side, The Minion strolls toward me so slowly that it actually gives my vision time to fully clear.

We're in the forest, at the end of what looks to be an old logging road. Fog hangs heavy. It's gray and moody out here, wherever we are. Brown, rotting leaves cover the forest floor. Three more vans, the ones that transported the remaining commandos and Deke are parked at odd angles off to the side.

I can only hope that we're not in the middle of a

dead zone and the GPS still works on my cell. Maybe that's why they didn't bother taking it. They knew it wouldn't help.

The Minion is short, like maybe five-foot-three in boots with thick soles, and he looks exactly like I expect him to look after all those appearances on television debating President Palmer over equal rights for superheroes. Insurance policies, right to life, you name it, they battled over it, metaphorically, during the election process. The Minion wasn't running for office, but he'd challenged both candidates to national debates in an effort to sway the vote one way or another. In the end, Palmer put on the best showing and made the most promises. He received The Minion's endorsement, and as far as I know, Palmer hasn't lived up to a single one of them.

Hmm. Should've thought of that before. Palmer made promises to SALCON that he hasn't kept, and, he initiates elimination procedures against its members. Double reason enough for The Minion to team up with George Silver.

The story behind The Minion is, he used to be a supervillain that supposedly "saw the light" and stepped over to do battle with the good guys. Could be true, because the guy has done a lot of good in the world for the superhero community, getting legislation passed, laws pushed through D.C. and whatnot. I can't say for certain if he's a double agent, but it seems to me that a lot more bad people fighting for the good side started showing up when he took over the office.

Regardless, I don't plan on trusting the guy to do anything for me, considering the fact that he'll likely try to murder me within the next few minutes.

The Minion saunters up, smiling, shaved head and a goatee rounding out the distinguished professor of bullshit look he's going for. His superpower is highly critical thinking—a brain so advanced that he once beat a supercomputer in chess in eight moves—and I seriously doubt I'll be able to outwit him in any mind games that he may try to play.

His dark blue suit is suave, and he looks like he stepped out of a Wall Street meeting where a bunch of fat rich dudes were laughing about controlling the world's economy.

"Leo," he says. "Good to see you in person. Do you mind if I call you Leo, or are we to stick with formalities? You know, I never really did like 'Patriotman' all that much. It rather tumbles off the tongue, wouldn't you say? Like a cinderblock inside a dryer."

"You can call me Susie, if you want."

He squints and shakes his head slightly. "Why would I do that?"

"Seems like it would be more appropriate for one little girl to get invited to another little girl's tea party like the one you got here."

The Minion clasps his hands behind his back. "I appreciate the attempt at humor, Leo, but you had to stretch entirely too far for the joke."

"Whatever. Look, Minion, what're we doing here? You got Deke Carter working for you, these goobers show up and take me for a ride in their party bus, and here we are. The only reason all of you bastards are still alive is because I'm curious."

With that, he cackles and howls with laughter. So do the rest of the SALCON commandos. That's fine. Let 'em laugh. He who laughs last, blah blah.

"I'm stumped, man. I've been pulled in so many directions over the past four weeks that I don't know which way is up."

When The Minion stops laughing long enough to answer, he says, "I have a hunch that you've figured out quite a bit of it by now."

"And how would you know that?"

"Once you really start processing things, it's easy to see that you're here for a purpose. You've had plenty of time to think it over, I'm assuming, yes? You knew Mr. Silver was lying to you, which is why you faked the death of Patriotman. You had to have figured something out, which is why you were at the home of our fine NSA leader. Rest his soul, he was a good man. Deluded, but I liked him for the character he showed. He made decisions and moved before they got cold."

He steps away from me, turning his back. "You recruited Polly Pettigrew or Kimmie—whatever her name is to help, so you had plans to do something, but I haven't figured out what just yet, and that usually means that you didn't have *anything* planned. Inaction, confusion, those are the only things that stump me, because if you have plans, then I can figure out where you're going before you do."

I don't say a word. I stare and let him keep talking.

"Now, the question is, which one of my two options will you choose, Leo?"

"What two options?"

"Oh, come now, you have to know that I have options available. Why waste a good resource?"

This is getting old. "Seriously, man, I'm not a mind reader."

His voice grows stern. "Do *better*, Mr. Craft. Challenge me! Show me you're worthy of being my opponent!"

I roll my eyes. "Here's where I see the game going, doucheface. One, you brought me here to kill me because you know that I hung up the tights as Patriotman, and I've been dropping the dirtbags that you've been enabling for all these years. And you want to know why I did it? You've let shitty, horrible people hide behind masks of justice while they go home at the end of the day and rub one out to snuff films.

"And don't give me that line about does it matter if the guy doing the deed is awful as long as the results are for the best. I don't agree with it, and I'm not buying it. Be good, be true, and fight with honor. Bad people do not get to say they're good just because they helped a little old lady across the street, and somebody had to do something about it. In fact, a bunch of us are—which I assume you already know—and that's exactly why Eric Landers is dead. Probably Joe Gaylord. Probably Conner Carson. There's a bunch of us out there cleaning up your mess, and it won't be long before your goobers here will try to take out the rest of them."

"Good, yes. Go on." He nods, smugly, and I'd like nothing more than to toss him into a burlap potato sack and sling him off to Jupiter.

"Two, I figure you plan to use me as a pawn. I don't know how you're going to go about it, exactly, but you've got your little lap dog Deke there helping George Silver inside of DPS. From what Deke says, one of their people, Charlene, she's gonna kill Palmer in a few days and somehow, you'll manage to lay that on me along with the death of Patriotman. Some nobody, like Lee Harvey Oswald for example, manages to kill two of the most powerful people in the world, and it'll be caught up in scandal and conspiracies from now until the end of time, and the government will feed the public some crap about how I was a loony that got too close. You know, for once, I'll be proving my own point wrong that it's usually the simplest explanation, not some grand conspiracy, because nobody will ever think to point fingers at the quote-unquote *good* guys. Sound about right?"

"Very excellent," he says, elongating the word in amused praise, the way a kindergarten teacher tells a student that his drawing of a tree is fantastic, and it doesn't look anything like a piece of poo like the other kids say. (No, that didn't happen *at all*.)

He adds, "My, my, my. I should've recruited you a long, long time ago. We should have, right, Deke?"

Deke crosses his arms and says, "For a meathead, he's pretty smart."

"Remind me next time to not be so…transparent."

The Minion steps closer to me. He smells like pepper and fabric softener. He leans in and examines my face uncomfortably close. I can feel the warm air from his nostrils cascade over my lips. This is how people must feel when they go to the optometrist.

I say in a hushed tone, "It doesn't matter what you do to me. I lost. I fell right into your brilliant little trap and you won. Pull the trigger and get it over with."

"All very good, Mr. Craft, and that'll come in due time, but you forgot one simple thing." He pats me on the head and yells, "Bring them out!"

TWENTY-FIVE

Present Day

I'm actually not surprised when I see someone emerge from the back of a SALCON assault van wearing a light gray suit with a red power tie, and the mask of a Doberman Pinscher. Frankly, I had been a little thrown off when George Silver, a.k.a. Suckerpunch, hadn't been hanging out with The Minion.

I'm floored, however, when I see that he's dragging Kimmie by her hair in one hand, and my poor mom in the other. Immediately, I lunge forward, and The Minion darts to the side, and this time, wisely, the SALCON commandos let go of me and allow the electro-bar to do its job.

I make it about a step and a half before the most violent shock I've ever experienced—even when I fought The Zapper it wasn't this bad—sends my body convulsing to the gravel road. I'm completely and entirely aware that I've lost all control of my bodily functions, but I'm unable to do anything about it as I lie here writhing. Thank the Good Lord, the only thing that happens is a stream of urine soaking my pants.

Whatever.

Humility went out the window eons ago.

A deep, guttural, "*Uuunnngggh*," escapes from my mouth when the shock stops vibrating through every atom in me. I gasp for air, listening to Mom and Kimmie scream in pain as George Silver yanks them around.

Damn, I can barely lift my head to watch. I groan and manage to get to my feet. "Oh, that's gonna leave a mark."

The Minion looks at my wet crotch and giggles like a kindergartner. "Looks like it already did."

Deke, who should probably change his name to *Dick*, stares at me with a pained expression on his face.

"What're you looking at?"

He shakes his head and glances away without a word.

Gordon looks so pleased with himself, I bet he has a boner.

George Silver shakes both my mother and my ex-wife. Mom is crying, and Kimmie looks like she's about to chew through bullets, but I can tell she's in pain. She's a damn superhero too—stubborn, mule-headed—but she knows that trying to fight back against so many goons isn't wise.

George Silver shakes my mother by the hair, and she yelps in pain.

I am so seriously, violently, all-encompassingly pissed off right now that for about thirty seconds, I can't focus on any of the words that are blathering out of The Minion's mouth. What I'm doing is sizing up my competition. Rage has blinded me to the point of eliminating all practicality. Before, I understood that going up against forty-five SALCON commandos by myself wasn't a viable option, but now, I'm thinking that if I can break this electro-bar quick enough to prevent too much damage, I might actually have a chance.

In truth, I'll probably get shot but I have to try.

Some of them are wearing helmets with goggles resting on top. Others wear balaclavas showing only their menacing eyes, staring me down, daring me to make a move. Kind of like The Minion, I can see a number of moves ahead, and I see a number of different options, yet the problem is I don't see a pathway to victory. There are simply too many enemies to mount an attack.

A sigh leaves my chest empty.

I feel it in my heart that this might be the end, and since the last time I've known defeat was almost thirty years ago, it's a dull, suffocating sensation that I'm not familiar with, and it only makes me angrier.

Mom and Kimmie are here for a reason. Leverage, I guess, and there's no telling what I'll have to do for The Minion to keep them alive a little while longer. I wonder how Phil's death has affected her. Does she know? Does she care? She better, damn it.

The Minion snaps his fingers in front of my face, bringing me back to clarity. I glare at him, blood boiling, and grind out a pissed off, "What?"

"I said did you hear me?"

"No, numbnuts. If I heard you I wouldn't have said, 'What?' And I thought you were supposed to be a super-genius."

Deke laughs at this. Good guy or villain, he's always gotten my sense of humor.

"Amusing," The Minion says, though it's not really, because I can tell that he's annoyed by my wit and Deke's laughter. "Sergeant Gordon, if you don't mind…"

This time I'm ready for the butt of his assault rifle. I duck my head to the side and feel it graze my ear. He shoves it at me again, and I dodge to the right. The minor jostling sends small jolts of electricity through my arms. It's not enough to hurt, however, and I continue to juke, dodge, and duck each of his attempts. He eventually growls and gives up, much to my amusement and even some of the tactical-suited goobers standing around me.

The Minion, annoyed and pretending to hide his agitation says, "At ease, Sergeant. Save your energy." He moves back to my twelve o'clock position again, and he's smart enough to stand out of my reach. He's small, rat-sized, and he knows that all it would take is for me to get my hands around his throat and jostle the electro-bar for him to be a goner. I can take it, but he'll melt like the Wicked Witch.

The commando to my left sniffles, and for some reason, it makes me hate him beyond reason that he gets to have something as *normal* as a cold. Oh, you've got a runny nose? How 'bout I snap your neck to help you out you son of a—

The Minion disrupts my mental murder by saying, "Here are your terms, Mr. Craft. First, I'm aware that Deke explained the plan to you, and I trust that you'll find it satisfactory for your colleague Charlene Templeton to assassinate President Palmer?"

"Go fu—"

"I'm not finished! She's quite capable, and once the deed is done you will accept your defeat and be branded as the man who murdered the President and one of the most beloved superheroes in history, Patriotman. Also," he says, beginning to pace back and forth, "you will have forty-eight hours to eliminate every single superhero assassin in your pathetic little support group."

"What? You're insane."

"Your people have been killing our people, you moron, and you should be ashamed of yourself for participating! How dare you, sir! How dare you kill your own kind!"

"And how dare you, you son of a bitch, for allowing perverts and murderers and thieves wear the masks of heroes! What is wrong with you—no, what is wrong with *society* when all you have to do is put on a nice face and you're worthy of an action figure that looks like you, huh? It's about character, you evil bastard. Be good *on* the field and *off* the field. You're only as good as your heart. A mask doesn't change that."

The Minion scoffs. "Oh, don't be so naïve. We don't live in black and white. It's not good versus evil. It's a hazy shade of gray that moves the machinery of life and people with antiquated ideas like yours are falling under the axe of progress. We can stand here and debate all day but it won't change a thing. The choice is simple; you eliminate the remaining superhero assassins, face a lethal injection for your part in the deaths of President Palmer and Patriotman, Eric

Landers, Joe Gaylord, Conner Carson…the list goes on. You don't know it, but you've been busy. You do this, and your dear mother and this little pixie might see a few more sunsets." He steps over to Kimmie and runs the back of his hand down her cheek.

Kimmie, awesome possum that she is, hocks a loogie and spits it in his ear when he turns away. Sometimes I miss her feistiness.

He wipes it clear with the hankie from his lapel pocket.

I say, "And if I refuse?"

The Minion shrugs and frowns. "It won't change much. You'll still be blamed for it all, and they'll die right here. Sergeant!"

Gordon spins around, as does Lewis, and one blink later, the barrels of their assault rifles are resting against the temples of Mom and Kimmie. Both scream. George Silver, who has remained eerily silent behind the Doberman mask, shakes their heads again to silence them.

"Okay, okay. Put the guns down."

They don't put their guns down.

"Put them down, I said. I'll do it."

The Minion starts to speak, but Deke Carter interrupts him by saying, "Nah, that won't be necessary, Leo."

What happens next is one of the most insane, diabolical, crafty, unbelievable double-triple-quadruple crosses in the history of history.

I can't make this shit up.

***

Deke Carter, agent of DPS, traitor to humanity, friend of The Minion, surprises all fifty people standing there, including me, when he pulls a white and lime green mask from inside his suit jacket and slips it over his head.

I recognize it immediately. The mask belonged to one of my childhood idols, and my God, I thought he'd died in 1973 when he fought Gargantuan underneath the Eiffel Tower.

Deke Carter is General Justice? You have *got* to be kidding me.

I don't have time to think about this or process it in any way, because he reaches around behind himself, pulls out a small baton and with the quick push of a button, it extends outward, metal wrapping around metal, clinking and clanking until it forms a colossal gavel the size of a warhammer. That must be some kind of nanotechnology insanity because that thing was no bigger than a hotdog a split second ago.

I think we're all in shock, because nobody reacts.

This happens within a couple of heartbeats, so maybe everyone is waiting to see what comes next, and it briefly occurs to me that Deke could be preparing to smash my head in and end it all right here. I don't flinch, not normally, but I do this time when he lifts the mighty gavel of General Justice over his head and swings downward…

…smashing right through my electro-bar, snapping it in two.

He's either saved us, or killed us both, and holy shit, he's not a traitor after all.

What the hell is—

I stand there, excited and perplexed as he bellows, "NOW, LISA!"

Huh?

Who I thought was George Silver in a mask responds by slinging my mother and Kimmie both to the ground and then in the same motion, reaches underneath the suit jacket and removes two semi-automatic weapons, crossed-arm style, and then slings them outward.

Two dull thuds later, Gordon and Lewis crumple to the ground.

What the—

Chaos.

SUPER

Deke, now General Justice, swings his monstrous
warhammer gavel and takes out four goons at a time.

Gunfire chatters as some of the SALCON
commandos turn on their own kind.

Traitors amongst traitors. Friends or foes, it's hard
to tell who is who.

I swing once, twice, three times, crunching the
ones standing beside me. Knocked out, dead, doesn't
matter, just as long as they're not shooting back. I turn,
frantically, making sure my mother and Kimmie are
out of the way. I can barely hear over the screams, the
gunfire, and the sickening thuds emanating from chest
cavities whenever General Justice lands a solid blow.

Mom is in the fetal position, head covered, and in
no immediate danger. Kimmie crawls, scrambling over
to her, and flings her body across my mother as a
shield. Beside them, a hand reaches up to remove the
Doberman mask, revealing Lisa Kelly.

Then where's the real George Silver? Dead?
Captive? Where?

I'm so thunderstruck that I'm distracted long
enough to feel a bullet part the air next to my ear. I
swing wildly, taking out everyone within reach,
grabbing a falling commando, using him as a shield.
Bullets ripple through him, and I use his gun to return
fire.

To my left, I see The Minion sprinting through the woods.

I drop low, assault rifle to my shoulder, and I aim.

I squeeze the trigger, and it's almost as good as an orgasm.

He goes down, grabbing his right butt cheek.

That's not where I meant to hit, but it'll do. He's not going anywhere. Not in a hurry, anyway. We'll catch him.

I'm up to my feet again, firing back at anyone firing at me, swinging fists and delivering thunderous kicks. I see Deke wrench to the right and grumble, taking a bullet, but who knows what kind of armor he's wearing under that suit or what kind of adrenaline he's running on—he's a superhero, after all—because he grunts, howls, and resumes dealing out justice.

Lisa fires and fires, spinning, twirling, dropping, and rolling like a ninja in a politician's suit. She's good. I have to give credit where it's due.

Soon, the SALCON commandos who are on our side have subdued the remaining soldiers. Deke buries his war-gavel one last time and stands up, holding his lower back and stretching. He's out of breath.

Agent Lisa Kelly rights herself, wiping the sweat from her forehead.

Kimmie rolls off my mother and stares up at the

sky, breathing heavily, then she gets up and brushes the dirt from her cutoff jeans. She rushes over to me, arms out, relief on her face.

Mom peeks out from underneath her hands and sits up. She stares at all the insanity around her and…and, well, she grins, too, which is just crazy because she seems a little maniacal and silly, like she either enjoyed it too much or she's gone off the deep end.

Everybody sort of looks at each other, bewildered that we've done it, that we were outnumbered and outgunned, and we survived. We don't need words because this is awesome.

Until it's not anymore.

As Deke strolls toward me, he glances over my shoulder and his eyes go wide in the cutouts of his General Justice mask. "Move!" he shouts.

Instead of getting out of the way, like he suggests, which would've been a smart move, my instinctual reaction is to spin around to see what he's looking at.

One of the SALCON commandos, who we thought was dead, is on his feet and bringing his weapon up to his shoulder. The voice that comes out doesn't belong to a man. "You really were kind of a prick, Leo. How does that make you feel?"

I can't quite place the voice, not behind the balaclava, but it's familiar.

Oh, Jesus, is that Dallas? I knew I shouldn't have—

And then the mask comes off.

It's Charlene. My mind has a second to process that she's yet another double agent.

She pulls the trigger as Kimmie steps in front of me.

TWENTY-SIX

Present Day

Kimmie's in a wheelchair, and, as usual, she doesn't want me to push her.

"I can do it," she insists, "and if you try again, I'm really going to kick your ass once I'm out of this thing."

We're walking down a small pier in Phuket, Thailand, where I'm in hiding until the superheroes who are pissed at me believe that I'm really and truly dead, or someone finally convinces them that my intentions were for the greater good.

A small, sun-browned girl chases a beach ball in front of us. Kimmie squeaks to a stop. She's making an excellent recovery, the doctors say, and if all goes well, she'll be resurrecting again as a new superhero within a couple of weeks.

I ask, "Have you given any more thought to what your new name will be?"

"Not yet. Any ideas?"

"Is The Cripple already taken?"

"Jerk," she says, but she can't hide her grin.

"How about Hot Wheels?"

"Getting warmer."

It's been good between us the past few weeks, and I can't help but wonder what it's going to be like once she's back on her feet. Obviously, Daddy Oilbucks could afford the finest nursing care on the planet if she wanted it. No, I'm here because Kimmie "suggests" that I owe her my life, and nursing her is retribution. The truth is, I kinda want to be here…just don't tell her that. I'm not sure I can take much more of her lording it over me.

We're connecting on a personal level, and I'm enjoying the fact that I don't have to fall in love with any woman who smiles at me.

I do owe her my life. She was trying to protect me. After three years of wanting to bury me, she stepped in front of a gun barrel for my sake.

You know how in movies, you always see people jumping in front of someone else to save their lives? Total bullcrap. It's one of the all-time biggest fallacies in movies. Human beings, superhero or not, are unable to move quickly enough to block a bullet.

Unless the timing just happens to be perfect, which it was. Kimmie took two bullets to the chest for me. One bounced off a rib, cut through the rest of her flesh without hitting any major organs, and then lodged itself in my hip. She wasn't so lucky on the other one. It ricocheted around inside, nicked a few things, and then damaged her spine enough to paralyze her from the waist down. She's strong, though, and to her benefit, she's been juicing her genetics with hyper-stem-cell injections for the past twenty years.

It won't be long now before she's kicking ass again. Her official pardon from President Palmer was announced last week, and she's promised me that there'll be no more backroom dealings with the Chinese. The thrill of fighting crime is more of an adrenaline rush than getting away with criminal activities, she says, and I'm glad she's finally learning that.

We come to a set of benches on the pier, and Kimmie asks if we can stop for a moment. "My hands are getting raw."

"I told you to wear those little fingerless gloves I got you."

"And mess up this tan? Are you nuts?"

"I know, I know."

She leans her head back, soaking up the sun, and I admire her long neck and those perfect breasts. You put her on the cover of a comic book along with all those other spandex-wearing ladies, she'd fit right in. She's bravely chosen to wear a white bikini.

Lately, showing off those war wounds in her chest are like a badge of honor, but the bullet wounds have healed nicely, and the scars aren't as deep pink as they used to be.

I keep insisting that it causes people to ask too many questions, that we put Bart Alonzo in a morgue for nothing, and people will discover that I'm still alive. I tell her that I don't want the secret to get out yet, not until I'm ready, and the only thing she says is, "You're just jealous that they're staring at my boobs."

She's right, but that's not my point.

Bart woke up in the morgue drawer a couple of days after our epic battle, and I had Sam escort him back to the Maldives. I think he's happier there anyway, and now that Sam set him up with a dark-skinned island girl, and I gave him my yacht and ample funds to retire on, he's living the good life. He swears he done working as my *doppelganger* but deep down, I think he has fun with it when I come calling. Some people like that element of danger.

Sam has been back in the States after visiting his family, and insists that he's ready to fully become Beast Machine. There's the matter of properly hooking up his armor, but he's close.

I look up from admiring Kimmie's recovering physique, past her and about fifty yards down the pier.

"Don't look," I say, "but he's still there."

And what does Kimmie do? She immediately looks and waves flirtatiously at the DPS agent, wearing bike shorts and a helmet, who's been trailing us for the past week.

He turns away, but not before shaking his head and smiling.

Deke and Lisa say that it's for our protection, that they want to keep us safe because we have work to do when we're ready. When I remind them that even though we're in hiding, we're still *technically* superheroes and can take care of ourselves, Deke chuckles and insists that the guy will only hover, nothing more.

I also remind him that they had a SALCON double agent among their ranks, and had no idea, and that I'm not entirely comfortable with another DPS goon being so close. "Don't worry," Deke had said, "I vetted him personally."

To which I'd replied, "Oh, just like you did with Charlene?"

He didn't have anything to say to that. He asked me to trust them.

I do, because he's General Justice, after all, but I'm relying more on my instincts than Deke's investigative skills. So far, Dork Shorts hasn't set off any alarm whistles.

Kimmie lifts her head and asks me to rub some suntan oil on her shoulders. Her repertoire of injections eats cancer like candy, which is why she has no trouble coating herself in what amounts to vegetable oil when she's in the sun.

I slather the gooey stuff on her and massage her at the same time.

She says, "I know you told me already, but I was wasted on painkillers. What was up with that Charlene chick anyway? You had a crush on her, right?"

"Now who's jealous?"

"No, I mean, if you had a crush on her, how'd you not pick up on something weird? Wait, never mind. I guess that answers my own question. You weren't thinking with the right brain."

"Exactly."

"Then how'd she end up in the support group thing? It seems like it would've been hard enough for her to work her way into DPS as an elite agent, *as an undercover SALCON agent*, then into your assassin group as a highly trained killer. How'd she pull all that off?"

"The same way that Deke managed to do it to SALCON and The Minion. You get good at telling lies. And it doesn't hurt to have a connection like George Silver who's playing both sides as well."

"I guess so. Sheesh." She glances out at the ocean,

then over her shoulder at me. "When does his trial start?"

"Six more months, at least, from what Deke says. Now that DPS has been thrust into the national spotlight, especially with that shithead Don Donner, they have to play by more rules. They can't sneak around in the shadows and pull everybody's puppet strings. Deke says they're lucky that Palmer let them stay on, but that's a thin-ice thing. He told me yesterday that Palmer wants him to head up the department now that General Justice is back, but he said no."

"Really? Why?"

"He's happier swinging his war-gavel than pushing papers. Feels too good to be behind the mask again, so they'll probably promote Lisa."

"She'll be great at it."

"Yeah." The plan, according to Deke and Lisa, is to pull all the members of SASS, the ones who want to keep that line of work going, underneath the umbrella of Direct Protection Services, considering the fact that Eric Landers, Joe Gaylord, and Conner Carson are all gone, God rest their souls. Plenty of bad guys remaining hidden under the masks of truth and justice, so for people like Tara and Mara, Don Weiss, and Mike and Eleanor, there's plenty of jobs left to keep them all busy for a long, long time. The rumor is, Ptera-Jackal, the new head of SALCON, is encouraging it. He's got a lot of cleaning up to do as well if he wants to get that cesspool filtered out.

Kimmie says, "I'd rather you work for her when you go back."

"If. If I go back. And besides, who says I'm *going* back?"

She raises her sunglasses and gives me a look that suggests I know exactly who says I'm going back.

"What? I'm having fun with you, playing invisible."

"Leo, really? You and I both know that there are hundreds of supers out there who don't know the truth yet. You're a traitor to them. The good ones want to kill you for betraying our kind, and the bad ones want to get rid of you for exposing their charade. And don't get me started on the supervillains, or that bastard Don Donner, because they've seen your face. Everywhere you go, you're a dead man, at least until some of this gets straightened out."

"That's why we pretended to kill off Bart Alonzo."

"*Pffft*. That was for the media. For the public. Our kind know. Trust me, they know."

"But I'm—"

"You know what your dad would've said."

"Phil or Bio-Dad?"

"Phil, goofball."

"He'd probably say, 'You're already an idiot, son, don't prove their point for them.'"

Phil. Damn it. The funeral was emotional. Mom cried. I knew she would. So did I.

"Precisely," Kimmie says. "Get it through that thick skull, honey. You are *not* Patriotman anymore. You're not Leo Craft, either. Those guys are dead and gone, and we're going to sweep the floors clean, invisibly, until it's time for you to resurrect. Got me?"

I nod. "Yes, ma'am."

"Good."

"Can I ask one more question?" I slide my hands down the front of her chest, between her Breasts of Perfection, which are the best superhero weapons of all, if you ask me, and then I gently caress her bullet scars. They're a constant reminder of what she did for me. I've been shot dozens of times and always begin healing on impact so there's no question I could've survived Charlene's last-ditch attempt before Lisa returned fire, but the mere fact that Kimmie was trying to protect me warms my heart in a place that I'd thought had grown dark. Sure, there were crushes and puppy love, and my inability to say hello to a woman without planning a divorce, but there was a spot

Kimmie would always occupy, and now there's light in there again.

She chuckles and shakes her head. "The answer is no."

"No what? You don't even know what I'm going to ask."

"I don't want to get married again, Leo. Not for a while. Let's see how this goes."

"That wasn't what I was going to ask."

Yes it was. That's exactly what I was going to ask.

Pathetically, I add, "I was gonna ask if you wanted some ice cream."

Kimmie uses her hands to roll away from me. She spins the wheelchair around and says, sarcastically, "You're such a horrible liar when you don't have a mask on."

She has a point. Given all the insanity over the past month, it's a wonder my trust issues haven't grown deeper roots, because whether you're a superhero or not, we all hide behind masks and tell the world what it wants to hear. When the masks come off, that's when you really see who is underneath. Hero and villain alike.

Or, in the case of Deke Carter, someone who you think is a real bastard can throw on a mask and become a superhero.

So yeah, I guess what I'm trying to say is, be careful who you idolize, but don't be afraid to give somebody else a chance. We're either hiding behind something on purpose, or we need to hide behind something to *have* a purpose.

Don't judge a hero by his mask, or some shit like that.

Patriotman, over and out.

***

Author's Note

Dear Reader,

So did you have a good time with *Super?* What a fun ride this novel was and I hope you had as much fun reading is as I did writing it.

Additionally, what you may not know is that I'm an independently published author (and a stay-at-home writer dad). I do ninety percent of the work myself, which means that I depend greatly on awesome readers like you to help me find and grow my audience.

Visit my website to join my free newsletter to learn when more fun books like this are coming.

www.ernielindsey.com

THEN

If you've enjoyed *Super,* I hope you won't mind spreading the word about it, and here are a couple of things you can do:

- Rate and review the book on Amazon. It doesn't have to be much, and even a couple of sentences can help sway a reader's opinion. You can make a difference! (But please keep Leo's surprise a secret!)

- This book is available for lending via Kindle, so share it with a friend.
- Tell your fellow readers about it on social media.

One of the great things about being an indie author is that I'm more accessible than some authors have a chance to be. Catch up with me on Facebook or Twitter and feel free to say hi.

Thanks for reading!
EL

Made in the USA
Las Vegas, NV
16 May 2021